HAWAI'I'S SPOOKY TALES 4

MORE TRUE LOCAL SPINE-TINGLERS

**COLLECTED BY
RICK CARROLL**

THE BESS PRESS

3565 Harding Ave, Honolulu, Hawai'i 96816
(808) 734-7159 fax (808) 732-3627 www.besspress.com

Design: Carol Colbath
Moon logo from a design by Kevin Hand

Library of Congress Cataloging-in-Publication Data

Carroll, Rick
    Hawaii's best spooky tales 4 : more true local spine-tinglers / collected by Rick Carroll.
        p. cm.
    Includes illustrations.
    ISBN 1-57306-114-X
    1. Ghost stories, American – Hawaii.
2. Tales – Hawaii. 3. Legends – Hawaii.
I. Title.
GR580.H3.C373 2000   398.25-dc20

Copyright © 2000 by The Bess Press, Inc.

The excerpt from "The Birth of New Lands," on page ix, is from Maud Worcester Makemson, *The Morning Star Rises: An Account of Polynesian Astronomy*, New Haven: Yale University Press, 1941.

ALL RIGHTS RESERVED
No part of this book may be reproduced or transmitted in any form by any means, electronic or mechanical, including photocopying and recording, or by any information storage or retrieval system, without permission in writing from the copyright holder.

Printed in the United States of America

In memory of Benjamin (Benny) Puakuni Keau, Sr.,
and Keith Kalani (K.K.) Keau, of Maui, who showed
me the way of the Hawaiian

Contents

Acknowledgments vii
About Rick Carroll viii
Introduction ix

Tūtū ....

Small Keed Time in Hau'ula • *Kenneth Makaio Hee* 2
Tūtū Man's Place • *Kamaka Brown* 19
The Grandma Who Talked to Ghosts • *Joyce Guzman* 24

Visions and Visitations ....

The Good News Dog • *Margo Howlett* 28
Nights in Old Kalaupapa • *Dion-Magrit Coschigano* 33
Pele Dream • *Pua Lilia DuFour* 38
Pat and Me • *Gloriana C. Valera* 44
The Night Pele Visited Hanauma Bay • *Dominic Kealoha Aki* ... 50

Spirits ....

Save the Life of J. D. Murphy • *Reney* 56
The Sunday School Teacher • *Aja Dudley* 62
A Moonlit Night at Anahola • *Joyce Guzman* 65
On Polihale Where Spirits Leap • *Angela Dollar* 70
The Old House on Kahuhipa Street • *Germaine Halualani-Hee* .. 75
Grandma's Finally at Rest • *Joyce Guzman* 81

Just a Feeling?

In a *Kapu* Cave • *Rob Pacheco* 88
Midnight at King's Landing • *Ronson Kamalii* 93
Phantom of the Ala Wai • *Susan Scott* 97

Rocks and Springs

The Power of Rocks • *Lee Quarnstrom* 102
The *Akua* of Kualoa Point • *Francis Morgan* 107
Grandma Brought Black Sand Home • *Brad Smith* 112
The *Kahuna* Stones • *Simon Nasario* 115
Kalaupapa Rocks • *Sunny Young* 118
Where the Hula Goddess Lives • *James D. Houston* 122

Sacred Places

Sacred Fishing Grounds • *Joyce Guzman* 130
Quest for Honopū • *Angela Dollar* 134
The Red Hand of Wahiawa • *Lani Donovan* 140

Heiau

Hawaiian Methods of Interment • *William Ellis* 146
Incident at ʻIliʻiliʻōpae *Heiau* • *Rick Carroll* 151
Something Awful Happened • *Rick Carroll* 158

Acknowledgments

As *Hawai'i's Best Spooky Tales* turns five, I must say thank you to all those who have made the supernatural a reality: to those who tell me stories and read these books, and those we can not see but know are there; to The Bess Press, Booklines, Bestsellers, Borders, and Barnes & Noble. And to the contributors to all five books, listed below.

Mahalo nui loa,
Rick Carroll

***Hawai'i's Best Spooky Tales: The Original* (2000; originally published in 1996 under a different title)**
Danny Akaka, Akoni Akana, Martha Beckwith, Burl Burlingame, Emme Tomimbang Burns, Ed Chang, Don Chapman, Lei-Ann Stender Durant, Leslie Ann Hayashi, James D. Houston, Mark Allen Howard, Phil Helfrich, Steve Heller, Nicholas Love, Bernard G. Mendonca, Gordon Morse, Victoria Nelson, Rob Pacheco, Mary Kawena Pukui, Nanette Purnell, Lee Quarnstrom, Pam Soderberg

***Hawai'i's Best Spooky Tales* (1997)**
Jay Agustin, Rich Asprec, Keala Binz, Cynthia Broc, Catherine Chandler, Micah Curimao, Nancy K. Davis, Darlynn D. Donahue, Helen Fujie, George Y. Fujita, Richard S. Fukushima, Bernard D. Gomes, Jeff Hitchcock, Ashley Kahahane, Hapa Koloi, Eugene Le Beaux, Tania Leslie, Linda Liddell, Alberta H. Lindsay, Jerrica Ann Keanuhea Lum, Sandy Martino, Gordon Morse, Gladys K. Nakahara, Lisa Okada, Lana T. Paiva, Kaui Philpotts, Mary Kawena Pukui, Kim-Erin Riley, Nicole Sarsona, Ed Sheehan, Ron Terry, Allen B. Tillett, Sr., Maureen Trevenen, Scott Whitney, Jason Wong, Dennis G. Yanos

***Hawai'i's Best Spooky Tales 2* (1998)**
Andrea Hunt Bills, Carolyn Sugiyama Classen, Thomas N. Colbath, Amanda Fahselt, Madelyn Horner Fern, Camie Foster, Helen Fujie, Nyla Fujii-Babb, Richard S. Fukushima, George Fuller, Joyce Garnes, Jeff Gere, Babs Harrison, Jerry and Debby Kermode, Alexis Cheong Linder, Ben Lowenthal, Ruben (Lopina) Makua, Chandelle Rego-Koerte, Stephanie Kaluahine Reid, Doug Self, Pam Soderberg, Shirley Streshinsky, Crystal Tamayose, Aaron Teves, Pat Leilani Young

***Hawai'i's Best Spooky Tales 3* (1999)**
Reggie K. Bello, Hannah J. Bernard, Suzan Gray Bianco, Robert W. Bone, Sonny Kaukini Bradley, Marcie Carroll, Carolyn Sugiyama Classen, Mary Ann Collignon, Maria de Leon, Ann Donahue, John Flinn, Nyla Fujii-Babb, Richard S. Fukushima, Steve Heller, Michael Hocker, Nicole Howe, Jachin Hsu, Claire Ikehara, Van Love, Charles Kauluwehi ("Uncle Charlie") Maxwell Sr., Simon Nasario, Kaui Philpotts, Michael Sturrock, Robert S. Tripp, Brian and Gigi Valley, Joana McIntyre Varawa, Robert Wenkam

***Hawai'i's Best Spooky Tales 4* (2000)**
Dominic Kealoha Aki, Kamaka Brown, Reney Ching, Dion-Magrit Coschigano, Angela Dollar, Lani Donovan, Aja Dudley, Pua Lilia DuFour, William Ellis, Joyce Guzman, Germaine Halualani-Hee, Kenneth Makaio Hee, James D. Houston, Margo Howlett, Ronson Kamalii, Francis Morgan, Simon Nasario, Rob Pacheco, Lee Quarnstrom, Susan Scott, Brad Smith, Gloriana C. Valera, Sunny Young

About Rick Carroll

Author and travel writer Rick Carroll is the creator of Hawai'i's Best Spooky Tales, one of Hawai'i's most popular book series. *Hawai'i's Best Spooky Tale 4* is Carroll's fifth collection of true accounts of inexplicable encounters in the Hawaiian Islands. He has shared these stories with audiences throughout the Islands in personal appearances at schools, libraries, bookstores, and conferences. He was a 1997 Visiting Artist on Lāna'i and performed at the Bankoh Talk Story Festival on O'ahu.

An award-winning daily journalist with the *San Francisco Chronicle,* Carroll covered Hawai'i and the Pacific for United Press International. His reports from the Philippines during the Marcos era won a National Headliner's Award for the *Honolulu Advertiser.*

Carroll's self-illustrated articles on Rapa Nui (Easter Island) and Huahine (Society Islands) have won the Lowell Thomas Award of the Society of American Travel Writers and the Gold Award of the Pacific Asia Travel Association.

Carroll lives in Hawai'i and Friday Harbor, Washington.

His next book, *Huahine: Island of the Lost Canoe*, is a true archaeological mystery about the only relic Polynesian voyaging canoe ever found.

Introduction

Angry flames shoot forth;
Redness grows, grows on the figurehead
Bounding in the ocean over there!
That is Aihi (Hawaii).

Land of raging fire
Kindling angry flames;
Land drawn up
Through the undulation of the towering wave
From Earth's foundation!"

—from "The Birth of New Lands,"
an ancient Polynesian chant

One night while sailing off the Big Island of Hawai'i aboard the SS *Constitution*, a vintage steamship full of famous old ghosts (it once plied the Atlantic and carried Princess Grace to Monaco and Ernest Hemingway to Paris), I awoke from a fitful sleep before midnight.

Seas were high, a general alarm was ringing, and I thought it must be a dream as I ran from my cabin fearing the worst. Suddenly, I remembered it was only a volcano alert. Only!

"All passengers report to the starboard side," a voice kept repeating over the ship's loudspeakers.

I joined what appeared to be a pajama party in progress—all the ship's passengers in sleepwear crowded the rail to see one of Hawai'i's greatest natural spectacles: red-hot lava running to the sea. Kīlauea volcano was erupting before our eyes.

The SS *Constitution* drew as near to the volcano coast

as the captain dared, and we stood in the balmy night watching the Big Island burn. It was frightening to see the mountain laced by veins of glowing redness, hear hissing explosions when lava tumbled to the sea, and watch a plume of toxic steam rise in exclamation.

I saw several Hawaiians aboard ship toss ti leaves over the rail. The ti leaves were offerings to Madam Pele, which I assume enabled us to pass safely and sail on into the night.

Even now, more than a decade later, events of that night haunt me; the sudden awakening to a ship's alarm, the hastily assembled crowd of pajama-clad passengers, the spectacle of a live, erupting volcano, and the ti leaf offerings which assured safe passage by the fiery shore.

A few years later the SS *Constitution* capsized in heavy seas and sank in the far Pacific on a voyage to India. No hands were lost, but it was a sad end to a once proud ship. I wonder if anyone on the final voyage had a ti leaf.

You can sail the Big Island's volcano coast on a cruise ship, and you should, for if your luck is good, and Madam Pele is dancing on the East Rift Zone, you will see "the land of raging fire"—one of Earth's spookiest sights.

You may want to bring a ti leaf.

In Honolulu you shouldn't leave home without one. Seems like there's always something spooky happening. The daily papers, often reputable sources of information, recently have reported stories that appear to have been torn from the pages of my Spooky books.

First, thirty-seven *iwi kupuna*, or ancestral remains, were "disturbed and removed" at a Kūhiō Beach water main project. Hui Mālama I Nā Kūpuna O Hawai'i Nei said the bones should have been left intact. The native Hawaiian community urged the Honolulu City Council to create a historic preservation commission. "The disrespect that is shown the *iwi* (bones) of our ancestors is unforgivable," said Shad Kane, a member of the Royal Order of Kamehameha I.

Then, big rocks started tumbling off O'ahu's North Shore cliffs, where ancestral burial caves abound. The rock slide closed circle-island Kamehameha Highway at Waimea, forcing construction of a $1 million emergency bypass.

When a boulder two feet wide fell on the *mauka* shoulder at Makapu'u on Kalaniana'ole Highway, Waimānalo residents grew alarmed.

"If it would have hit a car, it would have killed somebody," said Joe Ryan, a neighborhood board member. The State Highway Department began an investigation.

"In America, we don't give rocks much respect," *Honolulu Advertiser* columnist Mike Leidemann opined. "Maybe they're starting to take their revenge. Increasingly," he wrote, "rocks seem to be rebelling against the cold and heartless way we've treated them for so long. On the Pali Highway, at Sacred Falls, above Waimea Bay, rocks are striking out in dangerous, sometimes fatal ways."

Meanwhile, Big Island artifacts held in Bishop Museum since 1906 began to spread a mystery illness on O'ahu and caused a sudden death on the Big Island.

At least that's what the papers reported.

Museum staffers said they got the flu when they came in close proximity to a wooden female image; two *aumākua*; and two bowls, decorated with human teeth.

Discovered in a Kawaihae cave on the Big Island's

Kohala Coast, the objects were obtained by Hui Mālama I Nā Kūpuna O Hawai'i Nei, under the 1990 Native American Graves Protection and Repatriation Act. The artifacts are believed to have been reburied on the Big Island, where, according to the *Star-Bulletin*:

"Edward Kanahele of Hilo, a driving force in the move to repatriate the artifacts, collapsed Feb. 16 at a public hearing sponsored by the Department of Hawaiian Home Lands in Waimea on the fate of the artifacts. Kanahele, a founder of the repatriation group Hui Mālama, died in an ambulance on the way to the hospital."

Noted healer Papa Henry Auwae, who visited the cave, said the *ki'i* (images) are very powerful and very dangerous."

Those who believe in old Hawaiian ways know such incidents occur when graves are defiled, *kapu* broken, or certain island rituals ignored. News accounts only reinforce the fact that Hawai'i really is one spooky place.

Need more evidence? You've got it: twenty-nine first-person accounts guaranteed to give you chicken skin. Or your money back.

In this all-new edition of *Hawai'i's Best Spooky Tales* you will find true eyewitness accounts: peoples' stories about how and when they met Madam Pele, watched their pet dog become possessed, cast out evil spirits, endured haunted houses, experienced mysterious encounters, and survived unbelievable natural phenomena.

One of my great joys is to discover new voices of Hawai'i storytellers and share their work with you. It is my pleasure to introduce three new, never-before published Hawai'i storytellers, Kenneth Makaio Hee, Joyce Guzman, and Margo Howlett, who reveal a Hawai'i seldom if ever experienced by visitors or locals.

Introduction .... *xiii*

- Kenneth Hee of Hauʻula reveals the joy and terror of childhood on Oʻahu's North Shore in "Small Keed Time in Hauʻula, a spooky trilogy that includes "The Trophy Pig of Hālawa Valley," "Drop the Bone," and "The *Puka* of Hauʻula."

- His wife, Germaine Halualani-Hee, also contributed a very scary memoir about her days and nights in Kāneʻohe in "The Old House on Kahuhipa Street."

- Joyce Guzman, who grew up on Kauaʻi, contributes four hair-raising stories, three from Kauaʻi, one from Oʻahu: "A Moonlit Night at Anahola," "Sacred Fishing Grounds," "The Grandma Who Talked to Ghosts," and "Grandma's Finally at Rest."

- At Kahuku Library one night last October, Margo Howlett told me her mother gave birth to shark—and got my full attention. She then told me about "The Good News Dog."

Kenneth Hee, Joyce Guzman, and Margo Howlett have plenty of spooky stories, and I hope to share more of their tales with you in future editions.

Here are more previews:

- Dominic Kealoha Aki takes you on an overnight camping trip on "The Night Pele Visited Hanauma Bay."

- Pua Lilia DuFour's "Pele Dream" proves how spooky adventures of the dream self can be.

- "Tūtū Man's Place," by Kamaka Brown, which appeared first in "Hannabuddah Days," the online column he edits at alohaworld.com, is a haunting memoir of a Waimea Valley boyhood.

- Dion-Magrit Coschigano is a historian, an architect,

a film producer and definitely not a person given to superstition, yet strange things happen to her when she spends "Nights in Old Kalaupapa."

• *Honolulu Star-Bulletin* columnist Susan Scott didn't believe in ghosts either, until the day she met "The Phantom of The Ala Wai."

• Reney Ching of Honolulu offers a first-hand guide to an exorcism of a devil who possessed her pet in "Save the Life of J.D. Murphy."

• On her way to church, Aja Dudley, age nine, meets "The Sunday School Teacher," who appears from another era.

• Gloriana C. Valera describes the strange things that have happened in her family in "Pat and Me."

• Lani Donovan and her now ex-husband go guava picking on Oʻahu and encounter "The Red Hand of Wahiawa."

• Angela Dollar's "On Polihale Where Spirits Leap," and "Quest for Honopū" will make you think twice about going to the beach.

• Ronson Kamalii takes you with his Hilo pals to check out what really goes on around "Midnight at King's Landing."

• Sunny Young reveals what happened in Salt Lake when an Oʻahu neighbor imported "Kalaupapa Rocks."

• The late sugar planter Francis Morgan recalls the strange day he encountered "The *Akua* of Kualoa Point."

• Brad Smith learns a valuable lesson in "Grandma Brought Black Sand Home."

Introduction xv

Four early contributors *to Hawai'i's Best Spooky Tales* return with all-new chicken skin adventures.

• Lee Quarnstrom reveals "The Power of Rocks" in his O'ahu sequel to "Watched."

• Big Island naturalist Rob Pacheco takes you deep "In a *Kapu* Cave" and emerges shaken but unhurt.

• Simon Nasario recalls the O'ahu mystery of "The *Kahuna* Stones."

• And novelist James D. Houston takes you to Kaua'i, "Where the Hula Goddess Lives."

With bones and stones in the news, I thought "Hawaiian Methods of Interment," written in 1825 by London missionary William Ellis, might provide a right proper spooky insight to jolly old Hawai'i.

Finally, join me, if you dare, on an outing to Moloka'i's sacrificial *heiau,* where you will discover, as I did, what *waikōloa* really means in "Incident at 'Ili'ili'ōpae *Heiau*."

Still don't believe rocks have innate power? You will after reading "Something Awful Happened."

All who enter Hawaii must beware. Hawaii only appears benign. These islands are ancient and sacred and alive. Old bones surface, grave stones block roads. Madam Pele never forgets.

Go softly, be *akamai*, take your ti leaf.

Rick Carroll
Ka'a'awa, Hawai'i
October 2000

TūTū

Small Keed Time in Hauʻula

Tūtū Man's Place

The Grandma Who Talked to Ghosts

A girl is possessed by a demon. An old bone strangles a young boy. A *puka* opens in a banana patch. So many strange things have happened in Hauʻula, according to Hawaiian storyteller Kenny Makaio Hee, who in this spooky trilogy recalls the joys and terror of . . .

KENNETH MAKAIO HEE

Small Keed Time in Hauʻula

THE TROPHY PIG OF HĀLAWA VALLEY

I was just making eight years old when this happened smack in the middle of Hauʻula. We were living on Hauʻula Homestead Road, and a Portuguese family was living next to us, nice family, with a little girl, about five or six, very happy-go-lucky girl.

Her father was one big hunter. He used to shoot wild pigs, up in the valleys and on other islands, too. He was always hunting Molokaʻi—shoot animals all the time on Molokaʻi, deer, you know, for make venison, *pipikaula*, smoke meat.

One time he shot one animal, a big pig, over one thousand pounds, big story on Molokaʻi, big story. The people were very scared about what this Portuguese man had done.

One of the brothers up there in Molokaʻi said, "Eh, you know what, brah? You should just leave enough alone, just leave the pig, bury the pig, and go home, brah."

"Nah," the Portuguese man said, "I gonna take the pig back Honolulu. I spent all day tracking this big pig, finally I shoot 'em and kill 'em. So, I'm gonna cut off the head, keep the head, stuff the head, you know, make one trophy."

So he did, and he put the trophy pig head over the fireplace in his nice little house in Hauʻula.

Almost one year later, something very strange happened to the Portuguese family, to the little girl, Cheryl.

She got possessed.

I heard screams about ten o'clock at night like somebody was killing this little girl. I figure nothing. So next morning, the Portuguese grandma came over and talked to my grandma, who was into Christianity, she was a spiritual lady, too.

My grandma asked, "What happened last night? I heard the little girl screaming."

"I don't know, Annie"—that's my grandma's name—"I have no idea what's wrong with her."

So the day went on, we played, evening came, and the little girl got worse, she actually got sick, high fever. They brought in a doctor, in-house visit, couldn't find what was wrong with her. She got worse and they knew something definitely was not right but they couldn't put their finger on it.

My grandmother, she was a quiet lady, she was always observing things before she helped people. I asked her, "Tūtū, what's the matter with the girl?"

She said, "Never you mind, never mind, not for you to know."

So, our garage faced straight into the living room of the Portuguese family and, you know, I could see what was happening.

The second day, the girl is getting worse, she's terrible, she's foaming from the mouth.

The Portuguese grandma said, "Annie, Annie, I really

need your help. The doctors don't know what to do. I don't know what to do."

So my grandma said, "What you did?"

The Portuguese lady said, "Well, nothing to cause this. I feel one strange thing, but I cannot put my finger on it."

My grandmother said, "'*Ae*. You know what I gonna do? Call my elder"—which was my father's uncle. He's the pastor of a church. And so my grandma calls and explains to my uncle what was going on. She knew something wasn't right. My grandmother, she's talking to my uncle private.

Shortly after that, my uncle, the pastor of this church, he came over. They did their protocol, their *pule*, blessing themselves, reading the Bible—they read the Bible a good seven hours, reading and reading. And as they were reading, the girl got louder and louder. She started screaming, everything filthy.

Finally, my uncle said, "Annie, are you ready?"

They was ready to go, they left my house, they walked down the cement going around to the patio, and they tried to enter into the living room to this Portuguese family's house. They felt blocked. My uncle was pulling and pulling and finally he just pushed right through and they entered the house.

They could hear this little girl cussing—words I didn't even know the kine she said. "Get them out of here," she was screaming. The voice wasn't her—it was not this little girl. Finally, my uncle, grandfather, and *tūtū* entered into this Portuguese house.

The little girl, you could just see the *mana*, this evil inside her. My grandmother, I could see her in the living room, her hair literally standing up—black salt-and-pepper, Puerto Rican rough hair, straight up. The girl was screaming, screaming, screaming.

Just then her father drove up, coming back from the airport, and said, "Eh, what's happening?" and they told him, "Cheryl is—something is wrong with her."

When they entered the house, the little girl was literally floating, levitating off the ground. This thing had lifted her up like something holding her in the air.

So my uncle then—for an elder, he was tripping—he kept pulling and pulling and finally something released her and she just fell to the ground.

As my uncle approached, she turned around with a lashing tongue and cussed him. My uncle told us later she was talking in the devil's language. She was cussing my uncle from head to toe and my uncle was telling her: "The *akua* is the man, he is the kingdom, the power, and the glory."

He just kept saying that, and finally she came like a snake at my uncle and tried to bite his leg. And her father came, and grabbed her by her neck. I mean her father was big, he was huge, six-something, big Portuguese man, and he could not hold this girl. She threw him and he hit the fireplace with his head.

My uncle turned and he looked up and he seen this pig looking at him and he ask the Portagee guy, "Eh, where you get this pig from? Where you get this head from?"

"Oh, I shot 'em in Moloka'i," he said.

My uncle looked at my *tūtū*, and she said, "I, oh, I think—that's the stuff."

So, anyway, my uncle told the Portuguese man, "You

grab that head, get 'em out of the house immediately."

The Portuguese man never liked, there was something that was giving him energy for not listen to my uncle's words. And he said, "No, no, no no."

And the girl was going crazy. Things was flying, everything shaking.

Us little kids, me and my little sister, we listen to this and we just, you know, tripping out.

Finally, the girl's father said, "Okay, okay, I'll get the head and throw it out."

So he grabbed the head—the head wasn't mounted to the wall—and he had the hardest time and finally he handled the head, and he carried the head, and he opened the slider and he threw the head out and immediately it's like this whole spirit followed the head.

The girl—so emotional, sweating, fever, angry—she just went, "arghhg," and fell into a deep sleep. She slept for three whole days. Three whole days.

While she was sleeping, her father put the pig head in the fire pit outside. When he throw the pig head into the fire, this thing just made a strong noise and this bright blue flame and then a big red flame, and the head just disappeared.

My grandmother and my uncle said, "Okay, right now she's fine."

After the third day she got up. She never remembered nothing. She just does not remember anything. Her Portuguese grandma asked her, "Do you remember anything that happen?"

"No, Grandma," she says, "all I remember is these two eyes."

So her grandmother was explaining to her that what

her father brought back was *kapu loa*—no good. And our grandmother was telling us what was happening with this girl.

It was a trophy pig, all right. It was the sacred guardian, or *'aumakua,* for Hālawa Valley.

Next day, the girl came out to play and we looked at her like: Is she okay? And we was kind of scared for go play with her again. So anyway we finally played with her and she was doing the normal things again.

Drop the Bone

Okay, so three months later, after everything got calm down at the Portuguese family's house, me and my little cousin—I call him my *kolohe* cousin because the buggah, he no like listen every time—so anyway, he came over and we was playing around and my grandma told us, "Eh, you know, you guys no play in da bushes. Stay out of those bushes."

We looking at my grandma like, Why? Wassamattah in da bushes?

My cousin says, "Ah, crazy Tūtū, Tūtū's crazy."

But me, I know my *tūtū*. I see what *tūtū* talk about. I always did listen to Tūtū. My *tūtū* say no touch, that's okay with me.

Anyway, my cousin and I start playing in da bushes by Charles's house. And I run through the bushes and trip over this metal and find old train track.

My cousin, he's not too far from me, he's ovah dere pulling the whole sugarcane, pulling them up, playing with them, swinging them.

"Eh, put that down, brah. Grandma said, no play in da bushes."

I hear him go, "Eh, wow, what is dis? Hey, cuz, check out dis, brah."

I look over.

"What's that? Tūtū said no touch ovah heah. She know what she talking about."

My cousin, he digging some more, dig, dig, dig, and finally he pulls out this bone, this shin bone.

"Oh, look what I got."

"Eh, no touch that."

"Oh, it's a good weapon, come get one bone."

So he's swinging the bone around in the bushes.

"Cousin, put that back, brah."

He's swinging this bone around some more.

I try yell, "Tūtū, Tūtū," but, you know, too far, she no hear.

My cousin says, "Whacha calling Tūtū for? Come ovah heah she geev us one licking. Eh, look, anodda bone, brah. Grab da odda bone."

So, I looking at my cousin. "Go ahead, throw da thing down, go already."

As I walking, approaching him, yelling, "Get out of the bushes!" my cousin's walking and all of a sudden, "Arggghhh!"

Something grabs him.

"Arggggghhh!"

Something's got him around the neck.

"Arggggghhh!"

He's literally choking. He turning purple.

"Come, brah, let's go."

He falls down to his knees.

"Arggggghhh!"
He's really choking.
"Arggghhh."
I run up to him.
"Cuz, you okay?"
"Arggghhh!"
He's not okay.
"Drop the bone! Drop the bone! Throw the thing down."

So, finally he drops this bone. He gets up, holding his neck, catching his breath.

"Something was choking me. Let me go, already."

We ran back to the house. I tell my *tūtū*, "Tūtū, Tūtū, guess what happen to cousin?"

"What? He was playing in the bushes?"
"Yeah."
"He find something?"
"Yeah."
"What he found?"
"Oh, a bone."
"Ah, good, good, good for him."
My cuz look at me.
I said, "What? Tūtū nuts now?"
"Noooo, Tūtū right."
He listen to Tūtū next time.

THE *PUKA*

We were living in that Hauʻula house almost seventeen years. There was one neighbor I still remember, Mr. Freitas, nice man, very nice. We like play behind Mr.

Freitas' house in his banana patch. He got bananas, choke bananas. All neighbor kids go play in there, play hide-go-seek, play army, just like go in there.

My friend Charles, one day, he finds this *puka* in the ground. One big *puka*. And this hole was endless. What we did, as little kids, we throw things in that hole, I throw rocks and sticks and everything in that hole.

You know, you can predict how deep a hole is by how long it takes the sound for hit bottom. You go, "one, one thousand, two, two thousand . . . "

So, anyway I was going, "one, one thousand, two, two thousand, three, three thousand, four, four thousand, five, five thousand—wooo, da thing is still going—six, six thousand, seven, seven thousand . . . "

By the time it hits eleven, eleven thousand, I heard "whomp" and nothing.

Charles says, "Wooo, that's one big hole. Let's go check 'em out."

"I don't think so," I said. "I don't want to go down there."

So Larry—there used to be one adopted kid, Larry, Pākē kid—he like go chance 'em. He said, "You chicken, if don't go in the hole. Chicken shit."

I said, "No way."

So, he go down inside the hole. He disappear. We hear him.

"Hey, Larry, Larry."

"What?"

"See anything? "

"See nothing. Too dark. Throw flashlight."

So Jamie go grab one flashlight, go throw in the hole to Larry. We see the flashlight in the hole, going.

"Larry, see anything?"

"Nothing. Just roots from the tree on top."

All of sudden, we hear Larry scream. "Arggggghhhhhhhhh!"

"Larry, Larry, are you okay?"

No answer.

"Larry? Eh, Larry?"

I look at Charles. He looks at me. I said, "I'm not going in the hole."

Charles said, "Okay, I go."

We tied a rope to his jeans and tied the other end to a huge *kamani* tree, and Charles went inside the hole. And a good twenty minutes later he brought Larry back out of the hole. Larry was stunned. I mean Larry was in shock like he saw something, you know?

"Larry, Larry, are you okay?"

"Yeah."

"What happened?"

"I don't know."

"You went in the hole. And then you start yelling. And we never find you until Charles go get you."

"Oh, yeah."

"Larry, you okay?"

"Oh god! Is that a hole! Wooooo. That hole go far, brah. I don't know where this hole come from, but I look in the hole, I look real good, and I seen this devil. He was standing at the end of the hole, brah. And he look at me an' go "hehehehehe . . . "

"Then what happened?

"I wen' black out."

So we go get Mr. Freitas, tell him about the hole in his

banana patch.

Say, "Come, check out dis hole."

And he came over and as we are approaching the hole, looking for the hole, he said, "What hole?"

"Why, the hole was right here," I said. It wasn't there anymore. We can't find it. It's gone. Disappeared.

And Charles say, "It was right here. Look, because that's the rope. It stay tied onto the tree."

The spooky thing about this story is the rope was in the ground where the hole was. But the hole wen' close up on this rope. And you couldn't even pull it out of the ground.

I look at Charles and Larry, and Larry looks at us, and Larry's still in a daze, and Mr. Freitas say, "'Eh, you know, you keeds, you *pupule*. You need to go sleep early."

We look at each other, and Charles says, "This is where we was. We was standing right here, man. That's where the hole was."

It was gone.

We started to walk back to his house. All of sudden we heard a sound like scratching, scratching.

Charles say, "What's 'at scratching?

We see the rope like coming up out of the ground. And we see the dirt is falling back in, like something climbing out.

"Look! Look! Watch the dirt. Watch the dirt."

We standing there, watching and watching.

"Did you see what I saw?"

"I saw what you saw."

"You saw what I saw?"

"I saw what you saw."

So Larry go climb the huge *kamani* tree for get a better view. He's up in the *kamani* tree, looking.

"I no see nothing," he said.

All of sudden, the tree literally shake and Larry falls out of the tree, falls on his back. We run over there.

"Are you okay?"

"Oh, my back."

"What happened?"

"I don't know, brah, the tree wen' go shaking, brah, and I fall out."

He gets up, we help him up, and we look down by the river side, and I swear I see this ugly little—I cannot even say what it was—wen' go run by the rocks.

My grandma heard us talking about what we saw—the shaking tree, and the ugly little thing wen' go running off to the river, and the *puka*.

"What hole?" she said. "What tree? What t'ing?"

"Oh nothing," we say. "Nothing."

"What hole?" she said. "What hole?"

So Larry said, "Oh, the hole over there."

"You guys take me to where this hole stay, where it was."

"That thing gone already."

"No, no, no, you take me there."

So we go behind Mr. Freitas's house, take her to the hole. Where it was. As we approach the hole, my grandmother is already feeling this energy. She goes, "Oh, goodness, look at this, getting chicken skin."

She say, "Is this where you go play every day?"

"Yes, Grandma."

"I don't ever want to catch you over here again," she

said. "I slap your head, you hear me?"

So anyway, we walk in the banana patch. And she went up to where the hole was.

"Is that where you guys was?"

"Yeah, that's the one, but no more hole, Grandma."

She reached inside this plant, and she grabbed this fruit—it was purple—and she told us to get away, go. She took this fruit, and she threw it where the hole was, and it disappeared, it never hit the ground.

"Oh, Grandma, how you did that?"

"What you mean what I did? It was what's over there," she said. She pointed to the river.

"What? What you talking about, Grandma?

"I see that thing by the side of the river. What did it do?

"Nothing, nothing."

"I don't know what about this place, but this place no good. You guys get away from here."

She walked out from behind that place and we walked out and Grandma just stopped and started talking to somebody over near the river, somebody we couldn't see.

"Who's Grandma talking to?"

"'Eh, you bettah go," she said. "Nothing ovah heah, nothing for you heah, bettah you go now. Stay 'way from here."

"Tūtū, Tūtū, what you see, who you talking to?"

She grabbed me like this, around the neck.

"I told him if he knows what's good for him, he bettah go."

She took me to the house.

"Who you talking to?"

"It was him. It was him. In person."

"Him?"

"El Diablo, the devil. He's over there," she said. "He's standing across the river looking at you."

That night, it just so happens, it was a stormy night in Hau'ula. I never see Hau'ula so lightning, thunder, and rain, just slamming all one time.

I was in my room, lying on my bed, looking at top of ceiling, just dozing off, and I see this thing run across my ceiling. I open my eyes wide.

"What was that?"

Outside my bedroom window I hear something. I sit up in my bed. I open the jalousies up high. I no see anything.

"'Eh, what's that out there?"

Nothing. Nobody answers me. All of a sudden I see this thing walking. I shut the jalousie, I see this thing getting closer.

"'Eh, no come. I call for my *tūtū*, call my grandma."

It's one o'clock in the morning.

"Tūtū! Tūtū! Grandma! Oh, Grandma!"

And she no get up. She's a light sleeper, but this night she was just like something was put her to one big sleep. So anyway, she no answer.

And this thing is getting closer. I open my door, try go outside. As I try open my door, I cannot. This energy just pushing me back in my room.

"Grandma! Tūtū! Grandma!"

Nobody get up. So maybe I stay in the room. I turn to the window and this thing is right there by the window. I hate to talk about it—he's standing right there by my window. And he has long fingers and he's like hissing, li' dat, know what I mean?

I thought I was dreaming. I was ready for give up. All of a sudden my door flies open and my *tūtū* is standing right there. She looks at the thing and says:

"Go!" You know I told you. We have nothing over here. We have nothing for you. You go."

The lightning and thunder stopped, and a little drizzle started to come down.

"Boy, boy, come in my room and sleep with Tūtū tonight."

So I slept safe with her all night.

Next morning, she calls my uncle.

"Junior, go behind the house, get gasoline and . . ."

"I burn the rubbish already," Uncle said.

"No, go over there, I meet you over there."

She went to the back of the house, and I could see my grandma's hair float, no wind, but hair float.

"Ovah heah, by the boy's room, see . . ."

"See what? I no see nothing."

"Ovah heah."

"What's these red things?"

"That's what I'm talking about. Scoop it up, scoop it all up."

So uncle scoops up these red things and puts them in a pile.

"Is this what I think it is?" he asked.

"The buggah was here last night, Junior," my grandma said.

"Wow! I never see this thing in years," my uncle said.

I said, "Grandma, what is that?"

"That's Diablo's droppings, son."

"Junior, you put em over there by the pile of rubbish and you burn 'em."

"Hey, Mama, just bury them."

"No, burn 'em! Burn 'em!"

So Uncle makes five or six piles, piles 'em up, throws on the gas, and it was weird: the devil's droppings started to penetrate the gas, going off the wrong way.

"Light 'em! Light 'em!"

Uncle's still throwing on gas, so Grandma lights the match and she throws it on the piles. All of a sudden this huge, huge flame starts screaming, and in the flame was him: skinny, skinny-looking guy, and he's like hissing—you know da kine?—making this terrible sound. The fire was gone. Everything was gone.

It was awesome. I was just making eight years old.

Another family that I know living in that house now. And having kinda almost the same things. Must be something going on in the ground around the house. I go by that house sometimes. Every time I pass that place, I get the willies.

Kenneth Makaio Hee is a master storyteller who lives in Hauʻula on the island of Oʻahu. He is co-founder and aquatic *kumu* of Ka Lamakū Hawaiian Academy, which serves the children of Koʻolauloa. He is *a kahuna lāʻau lapaʻau lomi lomi ka koʻo* to *kumu lāʻau lapaʻau lomi lomi* Bula Logan, and a servant of Ke Akua perpetuating the spirituality and teachings of his *kupuna*.

Tūtū Man's Place *19*

Waimea Valley, up on O'ahu's North Shore, has been inhabited by Hawaiians since the day the lush river valley was discovered centuries ago. Archaeologists have identified 138 ancient burial caves and shelters tucked into the walls of the canyon. As years went by, Hawaiians were relocated, and their valley became a tourist attraction. When twilight fills the valley at sunset, Kamaka Brown, who grew up in the valley, can still see the ghostly outlines of . . .

Tūtū Man's Place

When you go to Waimea Valley choose a quiet evening near the river at sunset when the light is just right and the shadows from the mountains cast shadows themselves. Our valley remembers . . .

There isn't anything left of the house now. It's like you hear about the old neighborhood and how it's not the same. Well, 'most everyone has moved away to some place or another. Faces change like seasons. The trees have grown. We lived at Tūtū Man's place in the valley on the river.

I liked to walk down the dusty road that turned at the river when you didn't expect it to. Summer was the best time of year. The days were long and hot. Had choke fish in the river. The bufo frogs groaning their love songs in the cool of the evening across the water. Cows from the ranch would mosey over into the yard and eat Mom's favorite ti plant. She would get on the phone and call the ranch foreman. He'd drive down in his old Jeep like a movie sheriff and then come in for coffee afterwards. I never could figure out how he could fit those big feet with *puka* socks into those pointed boots with the run-down heels.

They filled in the low spots in the backyard. That used to be my hiding place. The hau *trees grew wild along the wall. That's where all my bad guys lived.*

In the winter the huge pounding waves in the bay closed the mouth of the river where it emptied into the sea. The river backed into the yard waist-high. Even the road to the falls was underwater! That's when I would climb on the wall and follow it to the twisted *hau* trees. It was "pirate time!" I would swing up on branches over the water like a pirate on the rigging of a bandit ship. Ooh, the adventures I had on the high seas of the Waimea River.

They had to use a tractor to pull the trees down. There is no trace of it now in the backyard except where it is safely tucked away in the video archives of my heart.

The *'ulu* tree grew along the tin fence by the falls road. You could tell the *'ulu* was ripe when the pinholes of milky sap would come out and drip down the side. We had one kerosene stove and Mom baked *'ulu* in it. She simply cut the core out and filled the hole in with butter and brown sugar. It's funny how the mind can store smells and tastes. Like coming home from school and smelling baked breadfruit in the oven. Eh, you can have cookies and milk; baked *'ulu* was "da bestest."

You could not mistake the smell of the river. It was brackish and ran green in the summer. From Halloween until New Year's it ran mocha. That was because in the wintertime the rains from the mountain would wash down the soil. The river changed mood then. It raged into a rapid with whitewater crests. Cows from the ranch sometimes got marooned on the piece of pasture that jutted out onto the river. That is when you could hear the waves thunder and feel the earth shudder with each set. We knew the river would soon overflow into the yard. That's when it was pirate time!

There isn't anything left of the house now. In fact, the homestead on the river is no more. The dispute in the courts over ownership of the land ended with the sheriff removing our belongings from the land and the bulldozers left to do their work.

Niimi Store, at the foot of Pūpūkea, was the place we would go for ice and kerosene. Twenty-five cents for a block of ice wrapped in newspaper. Mr. Niimi would get his ice hook with a handle to grab the ice. Hmmm, that would make a nice hook for pirate time.

Niimi Store is now Foodland, with electric-eye front doors that open when they see you. I liked it better when Mr. Niimi saw us coming and said: "Hello Mr. Brown, how your wife and keeds?" looking over the top of his glasses, and smiling. I don't think Foodland sells kerosene out of a 55-gallon drum, do you? The only ice they sell is in the bag, cubed. No need hooks for that, eh?

Nothing remains the same. I saw in the papers that part of the mountain fell on the Kahuku side of the Kamehameha Highway leading to the bridge and that they have built a temporary road across the sand for traffic. Auwē! *Everything has a purpose. My* tūtū *did say our valley get plenty* mana.

Under the coconut trees, if you look just right when the day turns to twilight, you can see a tin-roof house and a thicket of *hau* trees. If you listen carefully you can hear bufo frogs moaning forlornly, maybe get a whiff of baked *'ulu* in a kerosene stove, and on special evenings Daddy playing the guitar and Mom singing in her awesome soprano echoing in the caves and ridges of our valley, and there is laughter and the sound of children playing in the *hau* trees along the river at Tūtū Man's place.

Kamaka Brown, raised in Waimea Valley, Oʻahu, resides in Southern California, where he is a corporate trainer for a major telecommunications company. His passion is writing and stand-up comedy. He has performed on the West Coast and Las Vegas with Makaha Sons, Sistah Robi, Fiji, Dennis Pavao, Randy Lorenzo, and Hoʻokena. "Tūtū Man's House" is dedicated to his mother, Josephine Kamaka Duenas Jhun Brown, who died in Honolulu in 1999.

In Manila, in the company of doctors on an Aloha Medical Mission, I first heard the intriguing tale about how you could gain a dog's sixth sense by rubbing your eyes with a dog's tears. I thought about trying it myself but somehow never quite got around to making an actual test. I put the story in the category of "nice cultural myth" until I read Joyce Guzman's convincing childhood memoir about . . .

The Grandma Who Talked to Ghosts

Years ago, when I was in grade school, I had a friend who used to visit her grandma who lived in Puhi. Puhi is a very small town; if you blinked your eye, you passed it. The camp consisted mostly of Filipino families.

I remember that when Loretta came to school she would always tell me about her visits to her grandma's house. She knew her grandma was in touch with the supernatural and that things always happened when she visited.

In Hawai'i, there is a story told by the Filipinos that if someone puts mucus from a dog's eyes into his or her own eyes, this person would be able to see and hear the same things that the dog could see or hear.

Well, apparently, Loretta's grandma had experienced this. We all know that dogs seem to have a sixth sense. Sometimes we rely on a dog's reaction for anything strange happening around us. Loretta's grandma seemed to have this extra sense, and it became a torment; she never seemed to be able to stop fighting and arguing with the spirits.

One night Loretta's grandma was outside on the porch yelling and arguing with someone. Loretta looked out the window to see who she was yelling at. All she saw was her grandmother waving her hands, as if she were warding off someone away from the house, but there was no one out there that she could see. She finally came in and told Loretta not to go out on the porch—that she was telling the spirits to go away and to keep away from her house.

Loretta didn't know that her grandmother always put ashes on the porch, until the next morning, when she showed Loretta footprints in the ashes. Loretta said that sometimes she would actually see pots, dishes and pans flying all over the kitchen and her grandma still yelling at nothing in sight.

Till this day, I find it hard to believe that there could actually be someone who was not afraid of the supernatural and who would fight it too, but after seeing Loretta's grandma . . . .

She was something to behold. She had eyes that shined so mysteriously, and when she looked at you, it was a stare, a stare like she was looking right through you. I felt sorry for her, because I knew this woman was doomed to live the rest of her life warding off those spirits.

Joyce Guzman, born on Kauaʻi, graduated from Waimea High in 1961. She now lives in Dana Point, California, where she works for JCP as a makeup artist and sales associate. She also contributed "A Moonlit Night at Anahola," "Grandma's Finally at Rest," and "Sacred Fishing Grounds."

Visions and Visitations

The Good News Dog

Nights in Old Kalaupapa

Pele Dream

Pat and Me

The Night Pele Visited Haunama Bay

Poki, King Kamehameha's legendary dog, often appears on Kamehameha Highway on the Windward side of O'ahu. I've never seen the big white fluffy dog, but others have. Sometimes, they say, he runs alongside your truck, getting bigger the faster you go until he gets so big he disappears. Other times he just stands there by the side of the road. One night last October, while telling spooky tales at Kahuku Library, I met a Hawaiian woman whose family has had encounters with Poki as well as with . . .

The Good News Dog

Let me figure out how old I was. When I was living in Lāʻie my brother, Jimmie, went in the service at eighteen; he was in for two years. I was ten when he got out. He's exactly ten years older than me.

One afternoon, my auntie was driving us back to Lāʻie. We went to Kāneʻohe and we were on our way back, in Kahana. On the side of the road I saw this huge white fluffy dog walking.

At the time, I'd only seen a dog like that on television, the one on *Please Don't Eat the Daisies*. A big white fluffy dog, remember?

I kept staring at that dog because to me that was a *haole* dog from the mainland, and I thought *What is it doing here in Hawaiʻi?* We don't have those kinds of dogs.

I kept staring at the dog until we got around the corner and I couldn't see it anymore, but I couldn't stop thinking about that dog.

The very next day that same dog came into our yard, walked right into our house, and I recognized it. I was going, "Omigoodness, that's the same dog I saw yesterday."

Anyway, when the dog came into the house, we all

got scared, because my momma doesn't allow animals in the house. We were scared she was going to give us a good licking because we had this dog in the house.

Anyway, we tried so hard to get that dog out of the house. There were about seven of us at home. There's fourteen of us—I'm the youngest—but there were seven of us kids at home.

We got the broom and the rake and we tried to push that dog out and tried to poke it and everything and all it did was go behind the couch and sit down.

So we moved the couch out of the way and we kept poking and poking the dog so he would get moving and get out of there but he wouldn't move. He was so heavy.

All of a sudden my mom comes in from the back door.

"What are you guys doing?" she asked.

We all stood next to each other to block the dog.

"What are you guys doing?" she asked again.

We said, "Nothing," and she looked around and saw this dog sitting on the floor in the living room.

And she said, "Oh, leave that dog alone."

And we said, "What?"

"This dog just brought us good news. Leave it alone. Just let it go, let it go, move."

And so we all moved to one side. As soon as we moved, the dog stood up and made a complete circle around the living room, then went into the kitchen, made a complete circle, went into every single room, the back bedroom, bathroom, hallway, middle room, front room, and right out the door.

By then, because my mom had let the dog stay in the house, we wanted to keep that dog. We were all pulling its tail—"Stay here, stay here"—but he was so strong he just left.

My mother was in such a good mood, she just started prancing around the house and dancing and humming. And when she's in a very good mood, you can get her to say "yes" to anything.

So my brothers looked at each other and they said, "Hey, this a good time to ask Mom if we all can go to the dance tonight." And they asked her and she said, "Oh sure, just go. Just go."

Anyway, came that evening and everybody was getting ready to go to the dance. They said to me, "Don't you want to go to the dance?" Even though I was only ten, I was taller than all the girls then and I used to go to the dances with my family.

But I said, "No, I don't want to go."

"Why not? You always go."

"No, I want to wait for Mom's good news."

"Do you really think she's going to get something?"

"Yeah, I do."

Anyway, we were sitting down in her bedroom, looking at old pictures, and all of a sudden there was a knock at the door about eight o'clock.

She said, "Come on, Margo, there's my good news now."

We ran to the door and she opened it and there was my brother, my older brother, who had been in Thailand in the military for two years.

He wanted to surprise my mom. And there he was, and so she opened the door and she screamed, "Jimmie, I knew you were coming home."

"How could you know?" he asked. "I didn't tell

anybody."

"Oh," she said, "a big white dog told me."

Anyway, the next day my mom asked him, "What you want to do first?"

"Ah, man, I just want to have some Matsumoto's shave ice."

So my mom called my auntie and she asked, "Can you take us to Haleʻiwa? Jimmie wants shave ice," and she said "yes" and I went along too.

When we reached the Kahuku sugar mill, there on the left side of the highway was the big white dog.

My mom and my grandma always told us that if you see the colors white or red in a dream it means good luck. If you see black, then it's bad luck.

And if you see something three times in a row, it's really good.

I saw the dog three days in a row and it was so wonderful to see my brother again.

Margo Howlett was born and raised in Lāʻie, where four or five generations of her family also grew up. In fact, her ʻaumakua (Charlie, a shark) is from Lāʻie Bay.

Nights in Old Kalaupapa

For several years, work frequently took a Honolulu woman to Kalaupapa, home to some of Hawai'i's best spooky stories. It didn't take long for her to realize it would be good to find peaceful resolution concerning these ghostly tales, because when the lights go out it's very dark and lonely on . . .

Nights in Old Kalaupapa

Dion-Magrit Coschigano

Kalaupapa friends can talk story for hours about rolling balls of fire, armies of night marchers who "patrol" after dark, or the widow-woman ghost who dwells in a nearby sea cave.

It's easy to fall under the spell of these tales—I did the first time I stayed there overnight. That evening I'd been to a party at Marybeth's place, where we'd been entertained for hours with scary accounts of eerie Kalaupapa phenomena.

Later, as I was walking home alone, hairs rose on the back of my neck as I sped down unlit streets to the cottage where I was staying. Sensing dozens of night marchers right behind me, I quickly locked the front door and leapt into bed, muttering, "Now, stop it!"

A breeze blew in through the screened window above my bed, inviting drowsiness. Suddenly, a loud "thump" jolted me awake. A large nose shape emerged in the screen, pushing into the room.

Terrified, I pressed into the bed and watched the burgeoning outline and listened to its furious snorting. I don't know how long this horror lasted, but the nose—and noise—eventually receded.

When I finally found the courage to peek outside at

the "ghost" intruder, I saw a herd of wild deer moving through the yard. Night marchers indeed!

It wasn't long before I settled into the rhythm of Kalaupapa, accepting the ghosts and spirits of the community. There was no way I would allow superstition to interfere with my enjoyment of the place and the project that brought me there. For several years thereafter, my visits to Kalaupapa were undisturbed by the supernatural.

And then one night there came a late-night visitor . . .

It was the winter of 1992, and Kalaupapa was the final leg of a weeklong journey to all the major islands for a cinematographer and me. I was making a film about Hawai'i and had brought along the cinematographer to film sites and people. The two of us arrived at Kalaupapa on a stormy afternoon with barely enough daylight left for a brief reconnaissance of the areas we planned to film the following morning.

The week had been productive—but for an unpleasant discovery that the cinematographer had an aversion to visiting Kalaupapa, and frequently urged that it be excluded from the film. As producer, I felt equally strongly that it was an important element in the story of Hawai'i.

This passionate "discussion" continued on through dinner to settling in for the night in our respective rooms in the old visitor bunkhouse. "Good night," she snarled, banging shut her bedroom door at the end of the hall. "Good night!" I yelled back, kicking my door shut.

The bunkhouse is located slightly apart from the main village on an enchanting sea cliff where O'ahu's lights can often be seen. However, on that stormy night, nothing was visible and the building was surrounded by thick, sticky mud.

On weekends, the quarters are filled with visiting relatives and fishermen who often celebrate with songfests that rock Kalaupapa's quiet ambiance. On that night, we were the only guests, and our disagreement had created a stony silence in the five-room guesthouse.

As I fell asleep to the sound of rain, my last conscious thought was a hope that it wouldn't be too wet or muddy the next day to accomplish all the filming.

KA-BLAM! went the front door as it banged open in the middle of the night. I could hear someone very large with boots on striding down the hallway toward my room. The floor shook with each heavy step. I cried out "Who's there?" in a trembly voice while struggling into jeans and praying the flimsy bedroom lock would hold.

The cinematographer screamed.

Then . . . silence.

Except for the rain.

Slowly, I opened the door and looked into the hall. No one was there. The front door was closed. The wooden floor was without muddy footprints.

Impossible, I thought. Only a few hours ago we had to mop up the mud behind us when we came from outside into the hallway.

The cinematographer's door opened and she stuck out her head. We just looked at each other, without a word. Suddenly, she darted past me into my room, jumped into bed, and tightly pulled the quilt around her head and shoulders.

The following morning was bright and sunny, and we were able to shoot everything in time to catch the last

plane topside before sunset.
She never did speak of the event.

On the last day of an Island family vacation at age five, Dion-Magrit Coschigano vowed she would someday return and make Hawai'i home. She's lived on O'ahu since 1985. Enchantment with Hawai'i's sense of place led to work in historic preservation and to producing three films for the Hawai'i State Department of Education. She is currently writing a children's story about the pig god Kamapua'a and a screenplay that takes place in the Middle East in the nineteenth century.

When your dream self sets out to explore Hawai'i, you're along for the ride. You never know what will happen. Everything—adventures, characters, encounters—depends on what surfaces from your subconscious state. You have no control over your dream self, so you might as well lie back and enjoy the journey, as Pua DuFour did when she found herself in a . . .

Pele Dream

The day was bright; the sky was full of vog washing the sky gray. The air smelled thick and had a sense of foreboding to it. Birds were unusually absent and there wasn't a wisp of wind. Towering palm trees stood like sentinels watching over the sparse landscape, protecting it, holding it against the ferocious winds that can whip across the land at times. The sea glistened a brilliant turquoise, contrasting with the gray sky.

I found myself walking down a rock path toward a village. As I walked along, the sky began to darken ahead of me. Nearing the village I came upon an old woman sitting along the side of the road. She was bent and decrepit with stringy white hair. Wearing dirty rags, she looked like a beggar. There was something about her that gave me chills up the back of my neck. When I got closer, she looked up at me and asked for a drink and a cigarette. Her eyes were the color of coal.

I told her I didn't have anything on me, but if she accompanied me to the nearby village we could get her some water and probably find her a cigarette. She thanked me. I helped her up. She put her arm in mine. We began a slow walk to the village.

Nearing the village, we began encountering people.

The old woman asked each one she passed for a drink and a cigarette. She was met with derisive comments, pushed aside, and laughed at. Each time, she put her head down and muttered something under her breath. Then she'd turn back to me, take my arm, and we'd continue on toward the village.

Once inside the village we headed toward the well in the center of the square. The farther into the village we went, the more villagers stared, laughed and made rude comments toward the old woman. I felt angry and embarrassed for her. Once I tried to protect her. She reached out, took hold of my arm, and told me to keep my voice, that soon she would have her day.

When we reached the well, I got a drink of water for her first. As soon as she drank, I turned to get one for myself. As I drank, a hush fell around the square. I turned, and suddenly the old woman was gone and in her place was a tall beautiful woman with fire in her eyes, coal black wavy hair, and a foreboding frown. I knew this must be Pele. But how? What happened to the old woman?

She looked down at me, smiled, and touched my cheek, knowing my wonder. Then she turned toward the villagers and her voice sounded like thunder: "You ignored me and laughed at me. For that you will be punished." The villagers suddenly knew she was Pele, the goddess of fire, and rushed forward to kneel and beg forgiveness.

Ignoring them, she turned back to me and said, "Leave here quickly and never look back. There is a rocky knoll a short distance down the trail from here. Go there and wait. You will be safe there. Do not look back to this village as you leave or you will suffer the same as they do."

With that she vanished.

The people in the square began crying and wailing in panic. Suddenly they were running everywhere, trying to flee before Pele took her revenge. I left quickly.

As I was leaving, a loud rumbling began behind me. It grew louder and the ground began to shake violently. It sounded like thousands of freight trains rumbling toward me. I wanted to turn and look, but remembered her warning and began to run. I could feel intense heat behind me and knew Pele was exacting her revenge with fire. I saw the rocky knoll and headed for it.

As soon I reached the knoll, lava suddenly was all around me. I started to cry, afraid I would be dead within seconds. I raised my arms, closed my eyes, and pleaded with Pele to spare my life. Suddenly I was calm; I felt protected and knew I was safe and would live to see the sunset that day.

I don't know how long I stood with my arms outstretched. When I opened my eyes, I looked around and found I was alone in a sea of black lava. Everything was gone—the village, the people, trees; there was no sign of any life around me. Everything was wiped clean. It had become deathly quiet. Life had ceased to exist on this small spot of the world. Not even the wind dared raise his voice to the anger of Pele. The sun began to set, and the sky became a glowing orange-red. Watching the day end, I was suddenly at peace. Something amazing had happened, and somehow I was a part of it.

I watched the sun turn to cinders as it slipped over the horizon. I lost track of time and lay down to rest. I must have slept, because suddenly I felt something wet and cold across my face. I opened my eyes, wiped my hand across my wet face and looked up at a huge black dog standing over me. Around his neck was a golden flask. He licked me again as I sat up. The eyes of this dog were sea green and sparkled with flecks of gold that glinted in the light. It was as though you could fall into the depths of his eyes when you looked deep enough. This was the largest dog I'd ever seen, towering over me by several feet. When I got up, he nudged me and rubbed his neck against me.

I untied the flask, opened it, and smelled the contents. A sweet fragrance came to my nose. I knew it was safe. When I began to drink a voice came to me. "For your generosity and kindness I repay you with my drink. I have spared you and sent my devoted dog to aid you in your journey home. He is faithful and will lead you to safety. Heed him well, for he is my favorite. Thank you for all you've done and will do. You are in my favor."

I drained the flask and felt refreshed. As I looked at the dog, his eyes began to glow, and he looked toward the horizon where the sun had set. I suddenly knew how to get home.

I stepped from the knoll to walk in the direction he had gazed. When I turned to see if he was following me, he was gone. I was alone once again, but I knew where I needed to be. As I started on my journey home, the horizon started to glow purple from dawn approaching.

I rolled over and woke up. I was sweating, and my hair was matted against the back of my neck. Whew! What a dream!

Later that day, I discussed this dream with Auntie

Dalina. She hugged me long and smiled. "You have been blessed, Pua; use it for the lesson it is and remember, you are now Hawaiʻi's child."

Pua Lilia (Elise) DuFour now lives with her sea captain husband, Rod, and daughter, Courtney, in Friday Harbor on San Juan Island, her home away from home, in the archipelago of the San Juan Islands, Washington. She produces nature documentaries, writes occasionally, and spends her free time drawing, gardening, watching whales, and cooking. She enjoys beach barbecues with her friends. Pua believes the San Juan Islands are sister islands to the Hawaiian Islands, and that they have the same energy and feelings.

My sisters, Caren and Conni, are identical twins. They speak their own language, feel each other's pain, and often share similar experiences, although an ocean apart. Sometimes, siblings close in age also experience the same mysterious coincidences, as we discover in this haunting portrait of two intimate sisters, entitled . . .

Pat and Me

I want to begin by saying how my older sister, Pat, and I believe our late parents had some kind of extrasensory perception. We somehow inherited it from them.

Pat and I are only a year and a half apart in age. Teachers used to treat us like twins, choosing us to lead the Maypole dance or to dance a hula number as the school's program finale. We even used to play side by side as basketball or softball or volleyball players in elementary school and later with the Police Activity League in our teens. I'm a retired secretary-steno and Pat still works part-time as an insurance adjuster and secretary.

Our father, Florentino B. Virgeniza, was small in stature but very talented in sports. Born in the Philippines, he grew up on Moloka'i from age four, and retired from the pineapple plantation, where he was a truck driver and heavy equipment operator.

He once mentioned working night shift in the pineapple fields, which had a huge water tank. Whenever the workers had to fill their water truck, they would back up their truck so that the tank's water spout would be just above the opening on the truck. Then they would get out of the truck to turn on the tank's faucet.

Late one night, my father got out of the truck only to find the spout had moved to the opposite side of the tank. He backed up his truck again toward the spout, got out, and again saw the spout had moved to the other side. He finally realized what was happening and decided to leave the spooks behind!

Our mother, Emiliana Gashuman (Maui-born), was a housewife who always told us about her dreams. One night, she was dreaming that she was riding an airplane to Honolulu, looking out the window, and seeing her floating father wave good-bye. The next day, a call came from Oʻahu that her father had died of a heart attack.

By the time we were in our teens, Pat and I had already been experiencing incidents like reading each other's minds. We had moved to Oʻahu (Poamoho pineapple village) in 1954, and were still tomboys from Molokaʻi until we entered high school, where we made good grades and were shy, reluctant campus queens.

In 1969, after Pat and I had started our careers as office workers and later married, with one child each, our mother was diagnosed with cancer. The doctors gave her five months to live, and when that last day came, Pat was sitting in the optometrist's office while I was having lunch at my office at the airport tower.

At precisely 2:30 p.m., Pat stared at the clock, while at the same time I was sitting at my desk with a blank look, made a 360-degree turn to look at the clock on the wall, and immediately gave a deep sigh. Soon after, the phone rang, and I received word that our mother had died at 2:30 p.m.

Our father had been at the hospital, panicking because my sister's office told him she was at her doctor's and they didn't know his name. Grabbing the phone book, he turned to the list of optometrists and chose a doctor. The receptionist said, "Yes, we in fact have a Pat Cremer waiting for her appointment." All Pat had to do was run a short distance, because her doctor's office was practically next door to the hospital.

Eventually, our father moved in with Pat, her husband, and her only child, Brian. Grandpa was always around Brian: seeing him grow as a young soccer player or tuba player in high school, teaching him to drive around the neighborhood, and even, when his parents were away working late or on convention trips, checking in and reassuring him.

When Grandpa's heart surgery failed in June 1987, little incidents occurred at the Cremer's household for the next few months—or even till this day (their home is actually haunted). Pat and her husband would return from work, enter the house, and smell the sweet scent of gardenias, which were not in season. Our father used to gather a bunch of them and place them in certain rooms. Cigar smoke would permeate their family room downstairs. Our father used to smoke in the backyard. The rustle of newspapers could be heard every so often in his bedroom, where he used to read.

We believe our father's presence was strongly felt when Brian, then sixteen, was sleeping alone one night while his parents were away on the mainland on business. By that time Brian had a car and was always tinkering around in the garage, doing things like painting the wheels. That night he left a heating lamp on to dry the paint and forgot all about it.

Pat said that Brian was a deep sleeper, and they used

to have a difficult time waking him for school. That night, Brian was groggy, but felt a sensation like someone pulling his arms from bed, then pushing his back to guide him down the first stairway. When he got to the bottom of the second stairway, he opened the door leading to the garage and asked himself why he was there and how he got downstairs. To his amazement, he saw the hot lamp and immediately turned it off. Was that Grandpa who led Brian there to prevent him and the house from burning?

Another incident occurred between Pat and me in 1991. She had been coughing uncontrollably for almost a year, and I was always urging her to see a specialist. She kept saying her regular doctor was treating her and assured her she'd be fine soon. Her diagnosis later by another doctor was acute asthma. On a trip to Maui in mid-December, she woke up one morning hardly able to breathe. The ambulance was called, and just before she was wheeled out of the hotel, her husband, Mel, put one of his asthma pills into her mouth to swallow. The doctor at the hospital said that if it weren't for the pill, Pat would have been gone.

While all this was happening, I was feeling lethargic all day. On a Saturday, I usually slept in late, but that morning I was up early, moped around all day, and even missed lunch, which I normally don't. I didn't feel like attending our group of girlfriends' annual Christmas potluck that evening, but decided to go anyway. As I was leaving the house, I told my husband I wasn't feeling festive for the party. I usually wore a red outfit, but I ended up wearing black and white. When I returned home at midnight, my daughter said that Pat's husband had called at 9:30 p.m. to say she was at the hospital and had barely survived.

Till this day, I often wonder about the month of December. We almost lost Pat, and it was a few Decembers back that I recall a most eerie incident. For the holiday season, Pat had a desk against a wall with the top filled with rolls of Christmas wrap, tissue, Scotch tape, a large pair of scissors, and ribbons and bows. At the opposite end of the room, she was on the phone— talking to who else but me. She suddenly said nervously, "I am hanging up now and will call you back." She immediately ran out of the house to a park about a block away, where she calmed down for half an hour.

She called later to say her scissors were levitating about three feet above the desk! Would that have happened if our younger sister, Rita, or brother, Tino, were on the phone with her? Again, it seems mysterious things occur between Pat and me.

Born on Moloka'i, raised on a plantation on O'ahu, Gloriana C. Valera lives on O'ahu, where she is a retired office worker, housewife and mother.

Headed for Hanauma Bay on a midnight camping trip, when such innocent pastimes were still possible, two Kāneʻohe teenagers drive by an old woman hitchhiking on the highway near Sandy Beach and—ignoring Pele etiquette—don't stop to pick her up. In this riveting story, Dominic Kealoha Aki reveals, for the first time, the strange series of events that happened . . .

DOMINIC KEALOHA AKI

The Night Pele Visited Hanauma Bay

The night this happened, I was a junior at Castle High in Kāneʻohe, and my friends and I were going camping at Hanauma Bay. At that time you could camp down there, and many school groups and families used to camp there a lot.

We got a late start, and it was about 10:30 when my friends picked me up. We were just passing Sandy Beach out toward Hālona Cove, where the blowhole is, and on the *mauka* side of the highway where you enter the winding sea cliff road by the bus stop is where we saw her.

And she was in her old woman's form.

Apparently when she travels around the Islands, she appears in different forms—as a young woman dressed in red, or as an old woman dressed in white. Sometimes she appears as a fireball, a young child, or a small dog.

But this was an old woman.

She was about five feet one or five feet two, maybe one hundred pounds, and she had long silver hair down to her waist. She was wearing a white *pāʻū*, the skirt, and *kīhei,* the shoulder cover, both of tapa. She looked like she was in a toga outfit. She was walking with the aid of a cane.

As we passed her, she turned to look at us the same

time I turned to look at her. I still remember her face to this day.

That's an isolated road. No one travels that road at night except maybe a few fishermen or passing motorists. There's no one out walking around this deserted area of the island, not at that hour—about 11:30.

As we passed her I told my friend Steven to pick her up, but he declined.

He said, "I'm not stopping for anybody."

So I reminded him that if we didn't stop, it would be bad luck, and he said, "Well, that's not Pele."

"Of course, it's Pele," I said. Who else would it be?"

So while we were arguing this, we passed the turnout at Hālona Point.

And so he said, "Well, we've already passed the turnout. Besides, I don't believe those Pele stories, anyway."

As soon as he said that a big white bird flew in through the sunroof of his car—an old Capri. Sunroofs were real popular right about that time, real trendy.

Anyway, this big white bird flew in through the sunroof and started banging about in the car and we almost crashed—almost lost control and piled up. Steve pulled over and chased the bird out and we just stared at each other in amazement and were going, "What was that?"

"Eh, I told you. I told you. I told you. If you don't pick her up it's gonna be bad luck. You almost killed both of us."

He said, "That's coincidence."

"Coincidence? First off, you've seen the lady. We both agreed she looks like Pele, right?"

"Right."

"Right after you said you don't believe in Pele and you're not going to pick her up, did this big white bird fly in the sunroof?"

"Yes."

"Well, birds normally don't fly at night, do they?"

"No."

"I never saw a bird fly INTO a car at night, much less come in through the sunroof. We don't even know what kind of bird that was."

He said, "Oh, I think it's a seagull."

I reminded him we don't have seagulls in Hawai'i.

So he was going, "Well, it's just coincidence."

Anyway, we got down to the bay and told this story to our friends there, and they didn't believe us either. They went, "What? Are you guys crazy? What are you on? You guys drinking already?"

"Steve, tell them did you see an old Hawaiian woman walking along the road?"

"Yes."

"Did a big white bird fly in through the sunroof?"

"Well yes, that's true, too, but it's coincidence."

While we were arguing this point, one of the guys saw a golden light appear on the left side of the cliffs. (If you're down at the bay looking out, you see sea cliffs on both sides of the bay, with the bay in the center.) When we looked, the rest of us saw it too.

"What's that? What's that?" one guy asked.

"It's probably some fishermen," somebody else replied.

Then we all observed the golden light descend the left side of the cliff, move across the bay, ascend the right side of the cliff, and disappear into the night.

Around the campfire it got pretty quiet. Everyone was kinda spooked out.

"What was that?" somebody asked again.

"I think," I said, "that it was probably Madam Pele in her fireball form just letting us know, you know, that she's passing by this area to remind us to pick her up next time."

Nobody said a word. We were too spooked.

Because had that golden light stayed on the left side of the cliff—well, that could be fishermen up there. Or if it had gone down on the water, it could have been fisherman out on a boat. But when the fireball went across the bay and ascended the very steep right side of the cliff almost alongside the angle of the cliff—that was undeniable.

I wouldn't be surprised if we were the only ones who saw the fireball that night.

That's my true-life Pele story; it happened twenty years ago, but I'll never forget it.

Dominic Kealoha Aki is founder and co-owner of Mauka Makai Excursions, an eco-tour company specializing in cultural and archaeological field trips on Oʻahu. He leads locals and tourists alike to legendary cultural and sacred sites to see *nā heiau* (ancient temples), *kiʻi pōhaku* (petroglyphs), *kauhale* (house complexes), and *nā pōhaku* (sacred stones). His award-winning outfit has been featured on the Travel Channel and The Learning Channel.

Visit his web site at www.oahu-ecotours.com.

Spirits

Save the Life of J.D. Murphy

The Sunday School Teacher

A Moonlit Night at Anahola

On Polihale Where Spirits Leap

The Old House on Kahuhipa Street

Grandma's Finally at Rest

When her cocker spaniel started acting peculiar, as though possessed, a Honolulu woman took the dog for a checkup, but veterinarians could find nothing wrong. Her dog's strange behavior continued every night for weeks until an *akamai* uncle skilled in old Hawaiian ways helped . . .

Save the Life of J.D. Murphy

Reney Cheng

It began at three or three-thirty one morning about three years ago.

My little dog, J.D. Murphy, a purebred cocker spaniel, a gift from my sister on St. Patrick's Day, started acting real funny, running around in circles, chasing his tail, crying and whining.

I finally picked him up. He was trembling. I called his name out, kept calling his name out, but he was not reacting, not even looking at me.

So I took him outside. He couldn't move. His body was kind of stiff. I held him and tried to walk him around and called his name for a couple of minutes but he didn't respond.

Finally, slowly, he got to know I was calling him, but he was still trembling, not himself.

It was almost like something was around him, blocking him. I took him upstairs and held him.

I stayed up with him for about an hour. He didn't want me out of his sight. So I just kept him in the bed, and once he fell asleep, I fell asleep.

All this really worried me, so I took J.D. to the vet. He checked everything and found nothing wrong.

"He's not having any seizures, I can tell you that

much," the vet said.

Then, a second vet came in the room, and said, "You know, Reney, I really think there must be something else, a spirit maybe."

I could hardly believe that.

"Did someone in your family die recently? Or did you acquire something—a position maybe—that might make someone jealous of you?"

I couldn't think why anyone would be jealous of me or why that would have anything to do with J.D.'s behavior, so I just said I'd keep it in mind.

When I brought J.D. home and told my roommate what the vet said, we both were a little skeptical.

But then the behavior started all over again.

J.D. was running around, back and forth, chasing his tail, and this happened for weeks, about three or four o'clock each morning. And I got up with him every time it happened.

One time, it was just so upsetting. He was on the bed with me. I heard him crying, and he was going in circles and he just didn't know what to do, you know. He just couldn't settle down. And he was trembling and shaking and not responding to me like there was something around that he was more concerned about.

I talked to a cousin of mine, told her what was going on.

"Okay," she said, "you got to go talk to Uncle Eddie. He's real familiar with the Hawaiian spirits and the sensitive things that go on with our family."

I called his house and he said come over immediately.

So I went over and told the story to him and my cousin who lives there, and she got upset because she could really feel like something was happening. Her hair just stood up on her arms, and she said, "There's something we have to take care of."

"This is what you're going do," Uncle Eddie said. "I'm going to give you these two ti leaf hearts, tied in a knot. Put one in the bedroom, right where you sleep, and one near the entrance."

I said okay.

"You know," he said, "it's a spirit, a strong spirit, either a wandering spirit that recently passed on and doesn't know where to go, or a jealous type of spirit. I really can't pinpoint it.

"What you gonna do—because the spirit is gonna come back; I'm not sure when but it's gonna come back—get some Hawaiian salt and have it available in a plate and make another bowl of Hawaiian salt with water.

"When this incident happens with J.D. Murphy again, you need to get up and immediately take him to the front door or a near door.

"You're gonna open the door, you're gonna step back with your right foot and throw the Hawaiian salt with the water over your left shoulder and you're gonna swear and tell this spirit to get out of your life, and curse the spirit and you're either going to heal or something will just settle once you do that."

I said okay. I was really upset.

"Just relax," he said, "and just remember after you do that, take the ti leaf and go to the four corners of the house and just bless the house and pray, tell God to be with you, and use all the Hawaiian salt and keep the ti leaves in your house."

So I just kept that in mind.

It wasn't even twenty-four hours later when it actually happened.

I was in the kitchen and I had already made the two Hawaiian salts like my uncle told me.

It was approximately nine o'clock when my roommate goes, "Reney, he's in the living room, it's starting."

I came into the living room and, sure enough, it's like something had his tail and he was spinning in a circle, right by the front door.

I tell you I was so startled the hair was standing up on my arms.

I immediately grabbed the bowl with the water in it and opened the front door. I stepped back with my right foot and threw the Hawaiian salt over my left shoulder and said, "You bastard, get the hell out of my house." And I threw the salt over my shoulder with the water and I tell you it was like a little dust ball, I'm not kidding you—whooosh, whoosh, whoosh—it went right by my kneecaps and at that point J.D. collapsed.

And this is not a joke, I'm telling you, it was incredible, I just ran down the stairs, it was like instinct, I went to the four corners of the house, and threw the salt and I prayed and I told God, keep this away from us.

And ever since then we have not had a problem.

So I firmly believe in that, you know, and I keep those two ti leaf hearts my uncle gave me. I still have them, and it's been a couple years now, and J.D.'s okay, a healthy little guy. That happened when he was four, he's almost seven now.

Save the Life of J.D. Murphy *61*

Reney Ann Ching lives with her dog, J.D. Murphy, in Honolulu and owns Whirlwind Cleaning, a residential and commercial cleaning service. Neither she nor J.D. has encountered any subsequent evil spirits.

With images of god and angels and saints, churches are very spiritual places. Sometimes, religious spirits may even appear in broad daylight. Her mother says it's just a case of mistaken identity, but Aja Dudley insists that while she and her pal, Heidi, were on their way to church in Honolulu one Sunday, they both saw . . .

AJA DUDLEY

The Sunday School Teacher

This happened last October when my mom was cooking at our church, First Methodist.

Me and my friend, Heidi, were walking to the church, and along the way we kept seeing this girl, but we didn't know who she was. We would look back and see her and then, when we looked back again, she wouldn't be there. We'd look and see her and then she would disappear.

She had golden shoes, and a big white dress, and her hair was in a bun. She looked sort of like a Sunday School teacher. She was maybe about forty-something.

It happened five times, and then the next day, we saw her once in the same place—in my old Sunday School room. And then she disappeared and we never saw her again.

We were both spooked. We know we saw her and we know she kept disappearing on us.

At first we thought she was an angel, but then we thought not because she didn't have a halo or wings. We decided she was just an old Sunday School teacher from a time ago who visited our church.

Well, we tried to tell people, but my mom, she didn't believe me, because there were lots of people and she thought we might have seen somebody else and become confused. But we both saw her so it must be real.

Aja Dudley was nine years old and living in Honolulu when she shared this story. Her father is in the Navy, and she and her family are well traveled. Aja and her sister, Jordan, are home-schooled by their mother.

A Moonlit Night at Anahola 65

Instead of reporting to work at the midnight shift at the cannery, two young Kaua'i couples go *holoholo* in search of adventure and romance. At the end of a lonely road to a lighthouse on a seaside cliff, they park and begin to enjoy their escape from dull care until something spooky begins to happen on . . .

JOYCE GUZMAN

A Moonlit Night at Anahola

Dis was da old cannery days when you gotta get up early in da morning, like t'ree a.m., to get ready foah da girls to pick you up to go work carpool-style way up in Kapaʻa.

We lived about twenty-five miles away, an' dose days twenty-five miles was so fah dat da ride alone, plus all cramp up wit' like seven people in da cah, can 'come really boring an' uncomfortable.

One day, me an' Linda, my frien' who grew up wit' me from small keed time, decided we was going play hooky from work an' go *holoholo* wit' our boyfrien's. We nevah knew about haunted places in Kauaʻi, because we came from da west side, an' da east side was new stomping grounds foah us, especially when our parents so strict an' we no can go fah places. So we gotta sneak, yeah?

One day, we was suppose to work night shift, we had 'em all planned, we going all play hooky. All foah of us wen' wit' Mac's car dis time, Linda's boyfrien', an' we wen' to Kapaʻa, like we was going work, except we was going explore dis new territory.

When it got dark, we decide we was going dis place in Anahola, which we just happen to come across. Da moon was out, an' everyt'ing was so clear, you could see everyt'ing in da night, everyt'ing had beautiful silhouettes, trees, houses—you name it, it was beautiful.

So we wen' on dis road dat led to a small white bridge, really small dat only one cah can go at a time. We parked under some pine trees an' you could see like one big park or somet'ing, but we nevah knew what it was. (We latah found out dat dis was one ol' battlegroun' foah da ancient Hawaiians an' nobody goes deah at night.) Deah was one big white lighthouse dat we could see so clearly in da night, an' so we t'ought, "Oooh, dis a nice place to park."

Danny an' I sat in da front seat talking while Linda an' Mac was in da back seat talking. Dey decided dey was going walk outside by da watah—see, wheah we was parked, deah was pine trees an' den rocks, den da ocean, an' it was so clear you could see it like it was daytime excep' it was still nighttime.

As Danny an' I was talking, we suddenly felt da cah move like somebody was pushing or somebody big was leaning against it. So we looked ovah our shoulders on da right-side passenger seat in da back an' saw two big silhouettes, I mean really big. So we t'ought, "Oooh, was only Linda an' Mac," since they was wearing field jackets. So we nevah pay attention, t'inking was dem.

Suddenly, Linda an' Mac come running to da car, but from da oddah side an' wen' jump in so fas', dat had scare me.

I had ask dem, "Whatsamatta? You ac' like you had see one ghost."

Linda said, "Ey, shuddup you, I stay scared, somet'ing stay outside deah."

Den I wen' ask her, "I t'ought you guys was outside deah leaning against da cah."

She looked at me an' said, "Weah? ovah heah, neah da cah? Shuddup you, we was on da oddah side, ovah deah."

You should see all of us, we was so scared, t'inking Who da hell was dat den?

So Danny said, "Let's get outtah heah now."

Funny t'ing now, in Hawai'i wen somet'ing lidat happen, how come you cah no can start? Danny try turning dat ignition like crazy an' da cah still wouldn't start.

We kept saying, "Maybe if we sweah an' tell dem to get da hell outtah heah, maybe da cah going start."

All of a sudden, Linda says, "Ey, you guys see what I see?"

We all wen' look by da watah an' deah sitting on a rock was one *wahine* (mind you, she was transparent just like da ghosts they show in Disneyland) sitting deah wit' a sarong, long haiah wavering in da wind, her legs crossed wit' her hands folded ovah her knees while she looking at da ocean.

Linda was crying, da cah wouldn't start, we was SCARED STIFF!!!!

Da wind was blowing an' da pine tree was howling an' deah she was still sitting deah, we didn't know weah da oddah two "whatever dat was" were. We felt like we was surrounded by ghosts, stuck deah in da middle of noweah, in new territory foah us—man, dat was scary.

I told Danny, "Eh, leave da cah light on."

He said, "You no can start da cah wit' da light on."

Linda said, "I no cayah, leave da light on."

Mac started sweating an' guess what? Da cah wen'

A Moonlit Night at Anahola 69

START! We wen' outtah deah so fast, we had make tracks. Wen' we had get back to civilization (so we t'ought) we start to talk about it in da cah.

Mac said, "Ey, I gotta go hemo wattah," so we had stop by da pavilion in Kapa'a, an' no had lights in da bathroom. Linda had on her field jacket an' Mac had his on too, and wen Linda an' I wen' go to da *wahin*e side wit' no lights on, I bumped into her after we had make *shishi*, an' I had scream 'cause I t'ought was da big silhouette I saw by da cah. An' she had scream, I had scream an' we both start to cry. Da guys t'ought we was crazy.

So, nevah go places you dunno, 'cause you nevah know what you going come across in Hawai'i. I tell people here in California about ghost stories an' dey only laugh an' t'ink I'm crazy—boy if dey only knew, no?

Joyce Guzman, born on Kaua'i, graduated from Waimea High in 1961. She now lives in Dana Point, California, where she works for JCP as a makeup artist and sales associate. She also contributed "Grandma's Finally at Rest," "The Grandma Who Talked to Ghosts," and "Sacred Fishing Grounds."

Polihale Beach is Hawai'i's biggest; it's wide as three football fields and seventeen miles long. The gold sand beach wraps around Kaua'i's northwestern shore from Kekaha plantation town to 140-acre Polihale State Park, where Nā Pali coast ridge backs begin. The monster beach includes ancient *heiau* and burial sites, a view of the "forbidden" island of Ni'ihau, and night visitors, as Angela Dollar discovers when she spends the night . . .

ANGELA DOLLAR

On Polihale Where Spirits Leap

The first time I came to Polihale, I wept like a baby. There had been no terrible tragedy, no grave news or disheartening discovering. It was something else. The spirit of Polihale descended on me and brought it out. I had been warned. I wasn't prepared for tears to spill right out of me.

Since then, I've asked others about their encounters with Polihale. I was not alone. I have a friend who was so overcome with Polihale's energy that he did not speak—not one single word—for three days.

Another friend found himself running tirelessly on and on down the long beach until day's end. Yet another person described to me a feeling of being so struck by the power of Polihale, he spent his first days lying on the beach, in and out of sleep, unable to move. One can only imagine what sort of dreams he was having.

In Hawaiian folklore, coincidentally, dreams are a medium through which mortals communicate with the spirits of the dead—and learn from them.

On that first visit, sleeping out on the dunes, I had a dream that I was sleeping above an ancient burial ground. The dream was not threatening in any way; it was more a feeling that I was being informed.

Polihale, I have since learned, is considered the spirits' jumping-off place for the island of Kaua'i. Each island has one location where spirits of the dead are said to depart the physical world—the jumping-off place. After spending time there, I began to believe that Polihale is still open for business.

Once you become accustomed to the initial inundation of energy at Polihale, you get "in the flow," and it can be an incredibly powerful experience.

While Polihale moved me to sob big soulful tears, they came not out of grief; it was more like a cleansing. I never felt scared or endangered, just jarred out of my own reality. It strikes me as more of a gift to receive these spiritual transmissions from Polihale.

Polihale gives gifts to those deemed worthy. Each day, an array of beautiful shells washes up on the shore. Walking the long beach on a warm and dreamy morning, you may be able to collect enough *puka* shells to make a lei. The *puka* shell lei, in its sun-dazzled whiteness, gives the face of the wearer a regal glow. Then there is Polihale's crowning glory—the sunrise shell. A true natural masterpiece, its perfect scalloped figure is most often robed in vibrant pink, yellow, and white. Many consider it quite a fortuitous event to find one, though the sunrise shell seems more to find you. It is a gift from Polihale.

My friend Jim was thinking of the elusive sunrise shell one evening at Polihale and suddenly was gripped by an unseen force. He took off down the beach with his flashlight, and sure enough, came blazing back up to the campfire moments later with a brilliantly perfect shell. Finding this particular one, resplendent in a full array including blues, greens and oranges, was like finding a needle in a haystack. There's definitely something up at Polihale.

So what exactly is it about Polihale?

After numerous times of being called back to retreat there, none of us can pinpoint the sacred. We only know that when our campfires burn bright at night, it brings out the best in our storyteller's yarns and adds an angelic quality to our singing voices.

We know that the spirits are among us, and we often feel a sort of communication with them.

The natural world—the ocean, the sky, the stark cliffs rising behind the beach—seems to reach out and wrap you up. At Polihale one clear night I saw my first (and, to this point, only) moonbow. So serendipitous, yet the moon seems right at home over Polihale.

Sleeping out on the dunes at Polihale, I have awakened more than once and felt as if someone were watching me. Sometimes it's a mysterious, creepy feeling that pulls me down further under the covers, eyes clinched shut. Other times it is a warm feeling, one that is familiar and comforting.

I imagine spirits filing past me, toward the cliffs at the end of the beach, preparing to jump off into the immortal world. Keeping a respectful heart, I am passed by and not bothered. Yet I feel the wisdom and energy of lifetimes all around me, and I know I'm not alone.

Angela Dollar quit her job making backpacks in a small town near the Canadian border and set off to Kauaʻi to, in her words, "travel with the wind for a while. Every day here is a living adventure—a writer's dream." She has contributed articles to the *San Juan Island Sounder*, worked as a cocktail waitress in Skagway, Alaska, and continues to wander and write. She also contributed "Quest for Honopū."

The Old House on Kahuhipa Street... *75*

In a chilling childhood memoir, Germaine Halualani-Hee recalls a true-life nightmare in Kāneʻohe, the bayside town at the foot of the Koʻolau Mountains on Oʻahu's Windward side, where an evil spirit haunted her and then taunted her brother to death when they lived in . . .

GERMAINE HALUALANI-HEE

The Old House on Kahuhipa Street

When I was a young girl, I used to fall into trances. My Hawaiian grandma was a *kahuna*—I'm also Blackfoot Indian—and she told me early on, "You are like a magnet. People will come to you. You cannot fight it. They will always come to you."

The thing is, I wouldn't wish it on my worst enemy. It should be made into a major movie. That's how bad and scary it was. I mean it was total *Exorcist*-to-the-max.

We lived in a house in Kāne'ohe on Kahuhipa Boulevard. They used to have Hawaiian funerals there. Oh—the way Hawaiians mourn the dead: they wait for three days before putting the deceased into the ground. It was really scary for me.

There was a huge picture window. I looked in the picture window and I could see the silhouette of a casket and I was not able to breathe. "Help me! Help me! Help me!"

My brother came running down. "Wassamattah?"

"Tell me what you see."

"Nothing. I see candles."

"I see a casket and a Hawaiian lady, and she's sitting up in the casket, looking at me."

"Why are you scared? It's all family over there."

"I don't care. I don't want my family coming back to me like that. I want them stay in the ground and no come back."

Another day, at the front house in Haʻikū—there were three houses and the one in center was the focus of very, very spiritual activity—I see something, feel an arm go around me. "I like go home. I scared," I said.

"Why you scared?" my brother asked. "Just family."

"That lady standing in the doorway, looking at me. She smells like flowers. She's smiling, she's smiling at me."

He didn't see the lady.

Guess who? Came to find out, years later, we were going over family albums at family reunion and happened to come to this black-and-white picture and I go "Ahhhhhh. Auntie, who's that strange lady?"

And she goes, "Oh, that's who you named after—Kawailiʻula, that's her." And she says, "Why?"

"That's her." I said, "I saw her twice before, once in the casket, and once at the front house in Haʻikū."

She said, "'*Ae*, they had her mourning in the first house and they mourned her in the second house, and then the third day they put her to rest."

And she said, "She's only coming back checking on you. Only you get her name."

"I scared."

"You shouldn't be scared."

I'm scared of anything. I'm chicken. I am really scared only because I seen so much in my lifetime that I really cannot comprehend and I won't try to comprehend.

It scares me to death.

One day, when I was only fourteen, I met my husband-to-be. I told all my *kuleana* and he told me his. It was funny we should meet that way. I mean he had a lot of things to share and so did I.

"You, come my house and stay with me. I scared. My grandma got sick."

And he goes, "Okay I come stay with you"——but this time he didn't come my house. I kept calling him.

"I'm scared."

"What's the matter?"

"The doors are opening and closing ovah here. Open, bang, shut. Listen to this." I put the phone out and he listened for a little while and heard the noise. Like someone running around outside the house banging on the walls.

I said, "Please come," and I started crying.

And he said, "Where's your grandpa?"

"I cannot wake him up. Grandpa wouldn't get up. Please come."

Then I heard this thing calling me. I put the phone out again and my boyfriend heard my name being called by this thing, calling me by my Hawaiian name.

And this thing said, "Look at me."

I couldn't look at him. I was too scared to look at him. So I ran underneath the covers and started shaking and the lights grew very dim.

"It can't be happening. It can't be happening. I know it's not happening. I'm scared. "

I open up my blanket. I see this hideous-looking face. Trying to look at me through the blanket.

I couldn't scream. I couldn't breathe. I could smell his breath. That's how bad it was. The odor was like a decaying body, like a dead rat. I could feel his hot breath against my face and I went, "Omigod, omigod, oh please help me." I covered myself again. "This can't be happening. This is a lie, you know."

I opened it again and he was still there.

At that very moment I see my boyfriend running up the stairs.

And when he ran up the stairs the back door opens and slams shut—BAM!

"Tell me you saw him. Tell me you saw him."

"'*Ae*, I saw him," he said. "I saw him."

"I'm scared, don't ever leave me."

The next voice was my grandpa's.

"Geeee, what is all the noise?"

"Popppaaaaaa," I cried.

He goes, "I know. You no need tell me."

He went back in his room.

He knew.

This evil entity came back. He communicated with me.

"One day I will take one of you," he said. "I will take one of you. It's not you, because you belong to me."

It was too scary.

My brother, of all the people in the world, shot himself in that house.

I know how he came back from the other side, but that's another story on a different spiritual level.

He told me all he remembers is grabbing the gun and something standing next to him, saying, "Shoot. Shoot. Shoot."

My father is a witness. He heard someone egging on my brother: "I dare you. You are nothing. You nobody . . ."

And he shot himself.

The day he came back from the other side my brother said, "He dared me. I never pulled the trigger. I just held the gun and it just went off."

That's when I said, "We had enough, let's move."

We sold the house for real cheap, sold the place, and got out of there.

The new owner was having hard time building at that house. Every time he built with cement—big cracks. Even today that house is standing empty.

Germaine Halualani-Hee lives in Hauʻula, Oʻahu, where she is an educator and co-founder of Ka Lamakū Hawaiian Academy, which serves the children of Koʻolauloa. She is married to Kenneth Makaio Hee, author of "Small Keed Time in Hauʻula."

Grandma's Finally at Rest 81

Sometimes when people die they don't know it yet, and their spirit wanders around in a kind of daze until grim reality sets in. That's the only possible explanation for all the commotion one night in a house on Dillingham Boulevard, as Joyce Guzman writes in her eerie childhood memoir . . .

Joyce Guzman

Grandma's Finally at Rest

This was early in the '60s, when I was attending beauty school in Honolulu. I lived with my Auntie Rose and her family on Dillingham right across from Oʻahu Prison. My grandma used to come over and stay for a while, then went to the prison to visit my uncle, who was in prison at the time. I got to know her better by her visiting all the time and I liked being with her since I grew up in Kauaʻi and never had a chance to know Grandma that well.

Months went by, and she visited practically every day. One day when I came home from school, my Auntie Rose told me that my grandma had fallen sick. We took the bus and went to visit her in the hospital. I saw her sitting up in bed with so much pain. We didn't know what was the matter at the time, but I think they said she had something wrong with her stomach. She sat there trying to eat an orange that the doctor ordered, and all the while I could see the agony she was going through.

Grandma died soon after that. I felt so sad and helpless because I hadn't been able to do anything to help her ease that pain. My parents and sister flew to Honolulu for the funeral. Burial was at Punchbowl.

The scariest thing that happened was something I

don't think I will ever forget. While we were in mourning and having the nine days novena, I asked my mom if I could go out with my friends for a short while. She said that it wasn't right—that we were in mourning and that no one should be going out at this time. She finally gave in, and I left with Eddie to visit some friends.

As we were talking at Soly's house, I excused myself to go to the restroom. I was sitting there, and all of a sudden through the keyhole, which was directly next to my left ear (the restroom was so tiny that the door was practically in my face), I heard this voice in a whisper saying, "Go home . . . go home . . . ."

I looked at the keyhole and said, "Eddie, is that you? Hello, Soly, are you talking to me?" No one answered. I yelled, "Anybody out there talking to me?"

When I went out, they were all sitting in the living room and said that no one was talking to me. I realized that I shouldn't have gone out, and that it was Grandma talking to me. I asked Eddie to take me home and called my mom to meet me at the door. When I finally got there, my mom was at the front door waiting for me. She said to me, "I told you not to go out!"

The next night, when we were getting ready for bed, my cousins Rosie and Connie and my sister and I were in the kitchen with my mom because we followed her like scared chicks following a hen. My mom would say, "Why you guys following me around the house?" We all answered that we were scared knowing that Grandma had died.

Grandma's personal belongings, plus the cross that was on her coffin and was given to my mom, were all in the room next to our beds. The bedroom was set up so that one bed was across the way and two twin beds were put together, so all four of us could sleep together—Connie near the door, my sister, me, and then my mom. And next to her were Grandma's belongings.

We followed my mom from the kitchen to the bedroom and all jumped into our beds, waiting for her to get in. She kicked the door shut with her foot. As you all can remember, those days when you closed the door, some doors slammed and some just jammed to the floor, leaving the door ajar, yet almost closed. Well, this door just closed enough that it sat jammed to the floor. We asked mom not to turn off the lights, and she agreed.

All of a sudden, the door started to shake, then rattled so hard that we all looked at each other and started screaming. There was no wind, nothing to make the door shake and rattle like crazy. Connie, who was next to the door, flew across the bed and landed on me. Rosie, who was sleeping on the other bed, jumped across and flung herself among all of us. We started huddling close to my mom, all four of us, and my mom, who didn't know what was happening, said to us to calm down—that it was Grandma trying to get in. Like that didn't scare us even more! She then got up and opened the door and said, "I'm sorry, I didn't know you were behind me." With that, she left the door open and told us that Grandma's personal belongings were in the bedroom and, because she was so fond of them, she just wanted to be near them.

It was the hardest thing trying to sleep after that. We asked my mom the next day to please take Grandma's personal belongings to the other room, and soon after that Grandma was at peace. We never experienced anything strange after that. But remembering how that door shook with no explanation . . . .

My dad always told me that when people die, they are around for a couple of days, because they don't know that they're dead. He said not to be afraid, because they are your loved ones and they won't hurt you. When you are a kid, there are no explanations that can make you feel at ease, but I know now that it was only Grandma and that we shouldn't have been frightened.

Grandma's finally at rest.

Joyce Guzman, born on Kauaʻi, graduated from Waimea High in 1961. She now lives in Dana Point, California, where she works for JCP as a makeup artist and sales associate. She also contributed "A Moonlit Night at Anahola," "The Grandma Who Talked to Ghosts," and "Sacred Fishing Grounds."

Just A Feeling?

In a **Kapu** *Cave*

Midnight at King's Landing

Phantom of the Ala Wai

Hawai'i is a place that embraces. The islands have an energy that is warm, inviting, and familiar. The land seems to reach out and welcome you. That feeling is one of the many things I love about Hawai'i. Maybe it's because of this warmth of place that I was very much affected by an incident that happened to Rob Pacheco . . .

Rob Pacheco

In a Kapu *Cave*

Hawai'i is a place that embraces. The islands have an energy that is warm, inviting, and familiar. The land seems to reach out and welcome you. That feeling is one of the many things I love about Hawai'i. Maybe it's because of this warmth of place that I was very much affected by an incident that happened while I was caving a few years ago.

I have been caving for over fifteen years. Exploring the underground world is always fascinating. The Big Island is a caver's paradise. There are literally hundreds of caves on this island, all of them lava tubes.

A lava tube is created after red hot molten lava cools on its race to the sea and forms tunnels, caves, and subterranean caverns, often used long ago by Hawaiians as burial tombs.

For most people the idea of crawling on all fours in complete darkness as you descend is a spooky proposition. I have never felt that way. Though sometimes a particular stretch of passage can be difficult and challenging to get through, I always feel an adrenaline rush, as when playing a sport, rather than the threat of danger. In other words, I've never really been scared in a cave. Except one time in a cave in Kona.

I learned about the cave from a ranching friend. He said he went into the entrance a few yards until the cave got too low to walk in. He mentioned there was lots of air moving in the cave, which usually is a sign that the cave keeps going. What really interested me was that the cave was below a thick *'ōhi'a lehua* forest.

This meant the cave probably had roots dangling from the roof, which meant there was a good chance of finding cave-adapted creatures, troglodytes, such as planthoppers, crickets, and spiders. Troglodytes interest me, so I made plans to visit the cave.

Now I normally don't go caving alone—it's stupid. But I had it in my head to check out this cave on Saturday. My regular caving partner was unavailable, so I thought I'd just do a quick look-see to determine if the cave was worth a full-on exploration.

My friend's directions were perfect, and it took just a few minutes of hiking to find the entrance. The entrance was a small skylight with nice breakdown that allowed an easy climb down to the cave floor. The passage went about fifty feet and then began to get smaller; pretty soon I was crawling on all fours. But there was a good breeze coming through, and the air spurred me on.

After about thirty feet the cave opened up into a large room. At the other end of the room was a nice bore hole ten feet high with a smooth floor and lots of roots dangling down. Just what I was looking for!

I began to inspect the roots carefully, looking for the tiny, white, eyeless planthoppers or anything else I could find. Even though the conditions were perfect, there didn't seem to be any troglodytes on the roots. I slowly worked my way through the cave, and the roots got thicker and thicker.

Soon I was walking through a forest of hair roots; the passage was completely filled with these fine, moist strands. I felt a little bad, because it is not good for the roots or the creatures that live in them to be touched and moved, but it was impossible to proceed without pushing the roots aside.

Suddenly, I walked out of the roots and stood before a large lava pillar that made a fork in the cave. It was at this moment it happened.

I didn't see anything.

I didn't hear anything.

I didn't smell anything.

But I felt an unmistakable message: "You don't belong here."

At first I tried to reason with myself. *I'm feeling this way because I'm by myself.* But for the few moments I stood there, the feeling grew stronger. It was almost as if I could feel a pressure on my body.

Don't panic, I told myself.

I turned around and headed through the roots again. On the way in, I had moved carefully and slowly through the roots. Now, as a strong sense of dread overtook me, I rushed as fast as I could out of the cave. By the time I got to the large room, my heart was beating wildly, I was drenched in sweat, and I was truly terrified.

The whole time, I was trying to calm myself with rational inner speaking: *I'm fine. I'm only one hundred feet from the exit. There's nothing here. There's no reason to be scared.* But I was scared—terribly so.

I scooted through the crawl space faster than a cockroach. I scrambled up the breakdown and out into the sunshine in full panic. I have never felt such a sense of dread and hostility from thin air. I lay on the ground for several minutes and calmed down.

Normally, I would return to the cave with friends to explore and survey. But, I have no desire to go back. Just thinking about it gives me chicken skin. I still cave and have never had a similar experience.

I'm not sure what happened to me down there. The fear I felt was strange. It was more than fear. It was a message of urgency. It was like an alarm going off, with flashing red lights and deafening wails.

If I had to define the feeling, I'd say it was the feeling of *kapu*.

Rob Pacheco is founder of Hawaii Forest and Trail, an eco-adventure outfit on the Big Island of Hawai'i. His story "A Place Called Kapao'o" appears in *Hawai'i's Best Spooky Stories: The Original* (first published in 1996 under a different title).

Midnight at King's Landing 93

In "small keed" time in Hawai'i, you always hear stories about places to avoid, places haunted by night marchers, ancestral spirits, or ghosts of tragedies past. Sooner or later—it's a rite of passage on every island—you just have to go and find out for yourself what's really going on out there. Sometimes, the truth is stranger than fiction, as Ronson Kamalii and his Hilo pals discover one night around . . .

Ronson Kamalii
Midnight at King's Landing

I was born and raised in Hilo, Hawai'i. And like every other local *kanaka*, I would hear those stories about haunted places—stories that I didn't think were quite true, but was too chicken to question. Well, this is one of those instances where bravery ruled out common sense.

Back in my teenage years, me and a couple of friends would always go down to the beach to kick back and enjoy the environment—of course, also to drink some beer (legalities aside).

Every once in a while, we would talk about local ghost stories (or the thirteen steps in Honolulu that I encountered—somebody threw a mannequin on the road just below a hill, but that's another story . . .).

Anyhow, we started talking about a hospital that used to be at King's Landing up at the end of the beach road in Keaukaha—that it was washed out by a tidal wave and that at times you could hear the voices of the dead that used to be patients at this hospital, or, maybe, baby cries from the maternity ward.

Now King's Landing is a great fishing spot, and with the action of the waves crashing against the rocks, one could envision a tsunami taking out the whole area. So we decided to return to King's Landing just before midnight, to see if the stories are true. I guess amplification of astral voices is better at midnight, eh?

So here we are: It's fifteen minutes to midnight, and there's four guys sitting in a little Toyota Celica, under a tree, waiting for the witching hour to arrive.

We were all joking to each other prior to midnight, trying to scare each other prematurely. As midnight arrived, we sat in dead silence, ears acutely tuned to any audible sound that night. It was unusually quiet that night; the waves seemed to be distant sounds compared with the concentrated quiet inside that vehicle (mind you, we had the windows up—we ain't that crazy, you know).

As we counted off the chimes of the witching hour, just as the tenth chime went off, a cat landed square on the hood of the car, about a foot away from the windshield!

If you've never seen teenagers scream in fright before, it's not a pretty sight.

I was very surprised that my friend had the sense to start the car and high-tail it out of there with the cat still on the hood!

We never did know what happened to that cat. I think we used up kinda plenty of his nine lives.

Well, when it was all said and done, we stopped at the Dairy Queen down on Banyan Drive (we wanted to be sure we were well away, if you know Hilo landmarks). We parked the car and got out to stand around and look at each other, sizing up each other's bravado, and retelling what happened that night from four different versions.

My, what a life as a teenager in the little fishing village of Hilo.

Ronson Kamalii (Hilo High '80) now resides in Brandenton, Florida. After nine years in the U.S. Army he earned a bachelors degree in Environmental Science. He is licensed by the State of Florida to operate drinking water treatment plants. He works at a Reverse Osmosis Plant in Sarasota, Florida. He's single and enjoys fishing, racquetball, and reading techno-thrillers. His next trip home will be to visit his 'ohana and attend his twenty-year class reunion. He doesn't think a visit to King's Landing will be part of his itinerary.

Everyone expects to hear things go bump in the night, but when something out of the ordinary happens in broad daylight in a very public place, like Honolulu's Ala Wai Yacht Harbor, who knows what lurks there? In this mysterious tale, *Honolulu Star-Bulletin* columnist Susan Scott recalls the day she encountered what can only be described as the . . .

Susan Scott

Phantom of the Ala Wai

I enjoy hearing a good ghost story as much as the next person, but I must admit that during the telling, the logic circuits of my brain start overheating.

"Don't believe it," the scientific side of me usually shouts. "There's a reasonable explanation for what happened."

That's why my experience on my docked sailboat last week bugs me so much. I just cannot figure it out.

I was below deck using my laptop when I heard a huge splash near the boat. Certain that someone had fallen in the water, I rushed up the companionway and jumped onto the finger pier.

There, I saw water dripping from everything: the side of the boat, the pier, and the surf skis stored beneath it.

I stared into the water, waiting anxiously for someone to come bursting to the surface. All I saw were widening concentric circles.

I paced the pier. The area was silent and empty. Since the harbor is a big open space, no one could have heaved something into the water and gotten away that fast. I scanned the boat for a fallen part and checked the stored kayaks for slippage. Everything was in its place.

You might wonder why it didn't occur to me that a

marine animal had made a big splash. It did. But I have been hanging around this boat for years, and I know well the sounds of mullet jumping, turtles surfacing and schools of tilapia spooking. Also, I know the sound of someone falling into the water from the pier. This was that big of a splash.

My husband, Craig, arrived at the boat, and I told the story.

"Could a person sink to the bottom that fast?" I asked him.

"Susan, there is no dead body down there."

"How do you know?"

After some cajoling, I talked him into diving to the bottom beneath the boat. I figured that Craig, a better-than-average free diver, and a doctor, was a far better candidate than me for finding something awful down there.

He popped up. Nothing. I sent him back down. Finally, after several dives, he balked. "There is nothing down there," he said. "I promise. The silt isn't even disturbed."

Okay, so it must have been a marine animal. But what kind? I'll never know. But I do understand better now how spooky tales can get a foothold in the imagination, especially in the ocean, where we can't see what's going on.

So watch out for the Phantom of the Ala Wai. The truth is down there.

Susan Scott has written "Ocean Watch," a marine science column, for the *Honolulu Star-Bulletin* since 1987, and has written six books about Hawai'i's plants and animals. A registered nurse, she lives in Waialua with her husband, Craig Thomas, an emergency physician. Together, they volunteer each year to manage an Aloha Medical Mission clinic in Bangladesh.

Rocks and Springs

The Power of Rocks

The Akua of Kualoa Point

Grandma Brought Black Sand Home

The Kahuna Stones

Kalaupapa Rocks

Where the Hula Goddess Lives

In Hawai'i, many people, otherwise rational, logical people, believe rocks have special power. With rocks falling on the Pali Highway, at Sacred Falls, and above Waimea Bay, many people now wonder what's up. "Maybe, it's time we got in touch with our inner rock," a worried Waimea resident was quoted in Honolulu's morning paper. Or maybe it's time to begin respecting Hawaiian cultural beliefs, as Lee Quarnstrom recommends in . . .

The Power of Rocks

When the rocks started falling at Waimea, I knew what was happening but I didn't know why. Years before, I'd read that cliffs of Waimea held the graves of Hawaiians. When the rocks began to fall, I knew the ancestors were upset. I assume they're upset at all the traffic, all the noise, all the coming and going. But I know that rocks don't just fall in Hawai'i. There's always a reason. It has little to do with "natural" causes.

A huge wall of rocks slid across the Kamehameha Highway last March at Waimea on the North Shore of O'ahu. The rockslide closed the circle-island road until a temporary detour could be built across the beach to bypass the hundreds of tons of volcanic stone that blocked the highway.

The rockslide and the detour across the beach caused a big *huhū* in Hawai'i; it even made headlines in West Coast newspapers and became a topic of discussion among those of us who love and visit the Islands often.

"You hear that the Hawai'i highway department is going to leave those rocks alone instead of just bulldozing them out of the way and fixing the road?" a friend asked me the other day over lunch at a seaside bistro.

Our encounter took place in Santa Cruz, where my

friend spends about half his time. The other half is spent in a Turtle Bay condo. I was surprised that a man who loves the Islands and spends so much time there misunderstood the power of rocks. Let me tell you, that road at the beach where Waimea ("reddish brown water" in Hawaiian) Stream empties into the Pacific seems sacrilegious to this coast *haole* boy.

"Well," I told my friend, "Hawaiian public works engineers have different concerns than they do on the mainland."

Actually, I had recently driven across that beach detour, and with some trepidation—or chicken skin, as they say in Hawai'i.

It was disturbing to realize that we were driving not just across the sand at one of the world's prettiest beaches, but by a site of enormous historic and cultural value for Hawaiians, a place where the *mana*, or power, is so great that we'll all no doubt pay some price for its desecration.

The roadblock is probably only the beginning.

Locals, of course, know that the dead were buried in caves in the cliff. The bones are those of their ancestors, for God's sake. And for almost a century, writers have been reporting the burial sites.

J. Gilbert McAllister wrote in 1933 that "rock shelters on the face of the cliff . . . have been used as burial caves."

Didn't the highway builders know this?

Hawaiians knew.

They also know you're not supposed to build a road through what amounts to an ancient cemetery.

They weren't surprised when the basalt cliff thundered down onto the road tourists take to buy shave ice at Matsumoto Store in Haleʻiwa.

There are so many layers of *mana* and layers of reasons why the face of that stone cliff fell it's almost impossible to consider them all.

I like to consider the rocks, themselves.

Rocks, every Hawaiian knows, have *mana*. They have spirits. They have a certain consciousness that does not cotton to being disturbed, to being moved, rolled, dynamited, crushed, or otherwise blasted to smithereens.

When the road was first built at Waimea, rocks and stones from inside Kupopolo *heiau*, a small temple above the stream mouth, were taken for the roadbed, according to archaeologist Thomas G. Thrum, who wrote "Tales From the Temples" and *"Heiau* in Hawaiʻi Nei," in the early 1900s. Road builders broke away the stone steps, he said, and took many rocks.

Kupopolo, by the way, is not the huge Puʻu O Mahuka *heiau* overlooking Waimea and easily accessible by road. That huge temple atop the hill, once a *luakini*, or sacrificial site, is where three of Capt. George Vancouver's sailors, who went ashore for fresh water in 1794, were slain by Hawaiians angry at the intrusion by outsiders.

Yet another reason the basalt cliff was bound to tumble across the highway is that many rocks have special meanings, special powers, special symbolism.

The stones at Waimea hid burial sites and served as fishing shrines. The people of old stood on these stones watching for fish. A stone beneath Puʻu O Mahuka is known as Kalakū and, wrote McAllister, was a "patron of local fishermen."

Motoring around Oʻahu is more than a public works

problem.

It's a matter of respect for the dead.

In a place where stones have spiritual power and where the bones of the ancestors of present-day residents have been ignored or even disturbed by road builders, rocks are going to fall.

And highway engineers are going to leave sacred stones where they lie. Or ask their permission to be relocated.

They're not going to compound the sacrilege committed by the original highway builders by bulldozing sacred stones.

Or else.

Lee Quarnstrom is a writer in Santa Cruz, California. He is a frequent visitor to the Islands. He never disturbs rocks. His story "Watched" appears in *Hawai'i's Best Spooky Stories: The Original* (first published in 1996 under a different title).

On Windward Oʻahu at Kualoa Point, where the *pali* meets the sea just before Kaʻaʻawa Valley, a freshwater spring keeps everything green. Hawaiians long ago said the water comes from a cavern in the rock where an *akua* lives, but nobody really believed that until a young boy on horseback encountered what could only be . . .

FRANCIS MORGAN

The Akua of Kualoa Point

When I was a boy, still in high school and working on Kualoa Ranch, I rode a horse around Kualoa Point almost every day. To get from Kualoa to Kaʻaʻawa we had a narrow trail we'd go on, a horse trail just about where there's a horse trail now, but right close to the point where there's a spring.

Just above the spring was a great big rock about as wide as a desk and almost as high as the ceiling, the only rock around there, a great big rock, and the water trickled out under the rock and there was a little hole about big enough to put your hand in and the water just came out of the ground. We had it dammed up instead of just drizzling down the hill, and a half-inch pipe went down to a water trough for the cattle. A half-inch pipe just about took it all away.

So this old Hawaiian legend was told to me by my grandmother—you see my family has been here since 1850, and there were a lot of Hawaiians around in those days, and over the years my family picked up these legends—and my grandmother was the one who told me.

Apparently inside this spring there was a great big cavern—a big lake inside the mountain, big lake with big cavern and all these tiny holes with water coming out.

And they said that in there lived an *akua*, you know, a Hawaiian god, and he was kind of a benign *akua*, but every once in a while he'd come out. He didn't do any damage, but he just wanted people to respect him and to, you know, recognize that he was there.

And the Hawaiians said they could feel when he was out, and when they felt he was out they'd go put little offerings in this place where the water collected. And every once in a while I'd see them there when I'd go by.

It was just a little stick about like your finger, tied in a string or something with ti leaves, wrapped up not much bigger than your thumb. I never opened them up to see what was in there.

They'd say, "Oh the *akua*'s out," so they'd put the offering out and pay respect to him. So occasionally, I'd see these things and I never paid any attention.

I lived on the other side of the spring, and I went back and forth many times, and I generally rode the same horse, back and forth. I was working here on the ranch every Christmas and summer vacation, and weekends, all my spare time, and so what I'd do, I'd ride a horse back home for lunch about half a mile. Of course where I worked was all around, throughout the whole ranch, but most of the time on this side of the spring. I just went back and forth many, many times and I generally rode the same horse.

I was the only one who rode him. We had a real good relationship. He was a really good horse that did everything I wanted. He was just anxious to figure out what I wanted. So I didn't have to move much.

So one day I was coming over and—incidentally, another thing Hawaiians say is that horses can see spirits.

People can't, horses can. So if you're on a horse and if you can stay on the horse—don't get thrown off—you'll never get bothered by these spirits, because the horse could see 'em and run away.

Anyway, one day I was coming this way, and the horse came along the trail, just came to the spot and the horse stopped—wouldn't go. Same horse I'd always been riding, you know, so I got annoyed at the horse: "Hah, stupid horse, c'mon, go."

He wouldn't go, just refused, so I looked around to see if there was something odd. If there's something different, sometimes they get scared, like even if you have sometimes a rock in the ground, and somehow it gets turned over and used to be all kinda whitish and now it's black, ho! they get all scared of that, you see.

Nothing different, nothing different. Everything's the same.

So I just got really mad at the horse, just kept spurring at him and trying to make him go. Well, he just wouldn't go.

Finally, because I was pushing him so hard, he threw himself down the cliff—you know, below the trail—and it was a real steep place, nothing but bushes and stuff. The two of us, we went down. And I stayed on him, but we were crashing down, no trail, it was really a mess, and went below the spring. And I made him come up the hill the other side. Well, he came up—it was a hell of a struggle, but he did—and got back on the trail past the spring.

I thought *What the hell's the matter with this horse?* And so then when I went back on the trail I wondered, *What's the horse gonna do now?* But he was okay now that we were on the other side of the spring.

However, I looked in the spring and here were a bunch of these little tiny offerings, so I checked after, you know later on, and Hawaiians said, "Oh yeah, the *akua* was out and we went and put offerings in there."

So the only thing I can see is the *akua* was out and the horse saw him and wouldn't go. Nowhere at any other time has there ever been a problem with that horse going.

During the war, when the army built the road, and the tunnels where the guns are, they made a pile of rubble and they tossed it down the hill. It just covered up the whole thing. There's still that body of water in the mountain. A lot of times on the cliff by the road you can see a little green streak, even today.

Until his death in 1999, Francis Morgan, descendant of a *kamaʻāina* Hawaiʻi family, was the patriarch of Kualoa Ranch, a four-thousand–acre spread that runs from *mauka* to *makai* and takes in three valleys including Kaʻaʻawa Valley, where Hollywood filmed *Jurassic Park* and *Mighty Joe Young*, among others. A sugar planter, Morgan owned and operated the Hāmākua Sugar Company on the Big Island, one of the last sugar plantations to operate in the Islands.

The famous Black Sand Beach on the Big Island of Hawai'i, now buried under a lava flow, was an attractive nuisance. Ask any Hawai'i lifeguard. People scorched their feet and got terrible sunburns, and, sometimes, a rogue wave swept away the careless. But the beach posed other dangers, too, as we learn in this story about what happened when . . .

BRAD SMITH

Grandma Brought Black Sand Home

I must have been maybe ten or eleven when my grandfather died. My grandmother had finally talked my grandfather into going to Hawai'i on a vacation. She had gone before, and he had not, and, finally, they went together and, of course, they saw all the islands, did everything, the whole nine yards.

One of the things they wanted to see was the black sand beach on the Big Island of Hawai'i, which is no longer.

And, although she had been warned, my grandmother brought back black sand from that beach to the mainland. She said they had met some people on the beach who said you shouldn't bring back anything from the Big Island, at least not any volcanic rock. But it didn't seem like a big deal at the time, she said.

You know, it's real spooky, but within a year my grandfather died. My grandmother immediately took the black sand back to Hawai'i and left it there at the black sand beach.

It was, of course, after the fact. I do remember her many times telling us, "You know, you can't have that lava. I learned the hard way." That's her feeling, even now.

She told us about the black sand when I was in my teens; it just came up one day when we asked how Grandpa died. She feels that the reason my grandfather passed away is that she took the black sand.

I went to Hawai'i for the first time a few years ago. There was no black sand beach by the time I got there. It was all covered up by the lava flow. My grandmother now lives in Kona. She's in her eighties—I think she's eighty-eight now. She reiterated the story when we visited.

My sons wanted to take home a lava rock but, of course, my grandmother immediately intervened and retold the story about their great-grandfather's passing. She's learned a lot more about Hawai'i's customs, sacred places, *kapu*. So have we. You don't want to move rocks. Or sand.

When I go to Hawai'i, I never touch any rocks. Oh, I might pick one up and look at it, but I wouldn't have any thought to take it back with me. No sir, not me. I get a little shudder even now when I think about it. It's still spooky, even though it happened so long ago.

Brad Smith lives on San Juan Island in the Puget Sound and frequently visits his grandmother on the Big Island of Hawai'i with his wife, Kit, and two sons, Noah and Connor. They don't collect rocks.

The Kahuna *Stones* *115*

Years ago people came from near and far to Wahiawa to see a great stack of rocks Hawaiians considered sacred. One day, a plantation boss moved the stones to plant pineapple, and something awful happened. Pineapple's gone from Oʻahu now, but the stones remain, as Simon Nasario observes in this spooky tale about what happened years ago when *haole* planters tried to move . . .

The Kahuna Stones

Simon Nasario

While I was growing up in Hawai'i, I often heard the story of the *kahuna* stones of Wahiawa. They had magic power nobody could explain.

People came from all over the islands to rub their hands on the stones, then on their bodies, to get healed from what hurt or ailed them. People left all kinds of offerings—money and flowers.

We usually went there on Sundays. The place was always packed with visitors from all over.

I wonder if anyone today has ever heard the story of the *kahuna* stones. I don't want to give any wrong information, but this is the way I remember the story:

Eons ago a pineapple company wanted to put in a field just outside Wahiawa. So they started to plow up the land and came upon two stones. So the order was given to get the stones out of the way.

In those days, mules were used to plow fields. The stones were moved to the edge near the river.

Next day the stones were back in the same place, plus the mules died. And the drivers were very sick. The stones were moved again. Same thing happened.

So the powers-that-be in those days, after talking to

old Hawaiians, came up with the solution: Leave the stones where they were and dedicate some land around them for a graveyard. Nobody knew if it really was a graveyard, but that's what they said.

A chain-link fence was placed around the stones to keep looky-loos out.

Somehow, word got out about the stones. Soon people came from all over to see the stones, and they became famous as a place of small miracles. The story also went that if you visited the stones at night you could see the image of St. Joseph and the Virgin Mary with the Christ Child in her arms.

I don't know if any of that's true, because we never went there at night. Only on Sundays.

One stone was tall and slender and the other was round, not real round, but small with a cupped indentation on the top.

The stones were located in the pineapple field on the left side of the highway going from Wahiawa toward Kahuku. I don't know if the stones are still there, but I bet nobody ever dared to move them again.

Simon Nasario was born at ʻEwa, Oʻahu, where he also attended grade school. A 1938 graduate of McKinley High School, he served with D Company, 298th Infantry, from November 1941 to November 1945. A former ʻEwa Plantation worker, he now lives on the mainland. Nasario's stories "The Spirit of the Shade Tree" and "The Graveyard Shift in ʻEwa" appeared *in Hawaiʻi's Best Spooky Tales 3*.

University of Hawai'i philosopher Graham Parke says rocks are seen by Japanese and Chinese as "kernels of energy, fully invested with a life force of the universe." In Hawai'i, rocks often exhibit strange powers, as Sunny Young explains in this story about a neighbor in Salt Lake who imported . . .

Kalaupapa Rocks

In the first week of April of either 1990 or 1991, we had a rededication of our office spaces on the fifth floor of a Navy building at Makalapa on the island of Oʻahu.

The minister of Kawaiahaʻo Church came and gave the blessing. I thought that he was the minister who originally blessed our new home in 1985 (he was not, as I later found out from my wife); we subsequently landscaped the yard with a rock garden and fish pond.

The rocks came on a truck from somewhere else, and I began to wonder about the power of Hawaiian rocks, and if it was okay to bring these rocks into our yard.

I asked the minister if we should have our home blessed again. He asked me where the rocks in the garden came from. I told him I did not know. He then said, "Let me share a story with you."

The previous September, the Hawaiian lay minister at Kawaiahaʻo Church received a call from a Japanese lady living in Salt Lake and passed the call on to him.

The lady and her family had recently moved into a home in Salt Lake near the St. Philomena Church, which is in back of the Salt Lake Shopping Center near the library. (I was not able to determine whether it was a new house or one that they had just purchased.)

She stated that they were having a very difficult time staying there and requested his help. The family consisted of the father, who was Buddhist, and the mother, son and daughter (in their early twenties), who were Christian. The father agreed with the rest of the family to have the house blessed.

The mother said that at night they could not sleep because it seemed like people were walking across their roof and that the house was cold. (I've lived in Salt Lake for fourteen years and know it is usually warm there.)

The minister visited the home and entered through the front door. During the meeting with the family, the family was seated around the minister, on a couch and chairs. The minister commenced to pray with the family. Never in the conversation did he say that he was going to "bless" the home.

As he was praying, the daughter started to moan, foamed at the mouth and fell to the floor. As the moaning became louder, the mother pleaded with the minister to stop, but he explained that he must finish.

When the minister finished praying, the daughter was cleaned up and asked what had happened. She said that as the minister started to pray, she felt something pushing her into the floor and that she was trying to call out for help.

The minister said he then asked the family if he could look around. Just outside either the living or family room, he noticed a rock garden and asked where the rocks had come from.

The father replied, "Molokaʻi."

"Where in Molokai?" the priest asked.

"Kalaupapa," the father replied.

The minister then asked the family to return inside, where he prayed with them. Afterward, he told the family that they should not have further problems. About a week later, the mother called the church and said that everything was okay.

That's his story. I hope you can verify it with the minister.

As to having my house reblessed, he left that decision up to me.

Sunny Young and his wife Norma are both retired and now live in 'Aiea.

Go in search of hula origins in Hawai'i, and you will discover places at once sacred and magic, places of power and mystery, especially on the island of Kaua'i . . .

JAMES D. HOUSTON

Where the Hula Goddess Lives

I first heard about the hula terrace from a Hawaiian dancer. We were talking about the spell cast by certain modern-day performers, whose voices and supple bodies seem empowered from an older time. She said that if I wanted to understand the true sources of hula, I should visit this place called Kēʻē, on the island of Kauaʻi.

"It's mostly lava rocks," she said, "a kind of rocky platform out there by itself. It's dedicated to Laka, our deity of hula. You probably won't see any dancers. But you'll see where the dancing begins."

This was an intriguing idea, a very Hawaiian idea: that a dance tradition could be linked to a gathering of rocks, might somehow originate there. I had to see the place, and last fall I finally had my chance.

Though it isn't marked on many maps, the old terrace was not hard to find. Kauaʻi is a small island. There is only one road to the north shore. I followed it from the main town of Līhuʻe, up the windward side, bore west toward Hanalei, with its glistening taro ponds, and on past Lumahaʻi Beach, where they filmed scenes from *South Pacific*. Out that way razor-topped canyons notch the shoreline. About a mile past Hāʻena, the most northerly point in the main Hawaiian chain, the road ends at a sandy little cove called Kē'ē Beach.

From there, as the dancer had instructed me to do, I hiked along the shore for one hundred yards or so. Beyond the last house on that side of the island, a wet path cuts inland through pandanus thicket. Nothing marks the route until you have climbed awhile and come upon a simple sign saying, Ka-Ulu-Paoa-Heiau. *Heiau* means "place of worship." Paoa had been a famous priest in this region. The corner of an old foundation loomed above me, the remains of the temple named for him, now a sloping stack of lava rocks.

Climbing out of the trees I saw that a whole hillside had once been terraced with rock embankments rising from the temple toward a small plateau. On this uppermost level I found the platform, a rock-bordered and grassy rectangle, at the foot of a stone cliff splotched white with lichen.

It is called Ka-Ulu-O-Laka Hālau Hula. *Hālau* means a "long house or meeting place." *Ulu* means "to grow or increase," as well as "to be artistically inspired by a god or spirit." Thus: A Place of Dance Honoring the Inspiration of Laka.

Whenever I come upon one of these revered Hawaiian sites, I have learned to stand still awhile and listen and look around. Why here? I ask myself. Why not closer to the beach? Or at the top of this cliff? Or across that ravine? There is always some appropriate mix of features that gives the spot its own appeal and holding power.

In the case of Kē'ē, it is important to bear in mind that hula in early Hawai'i was much more than a form of entertainment. For dancers it was a sacred calling, to which you dedicated your life. Hawaiians had no written language. Chanters and dancers were the poets, historians and keepers of the flame.

Hands and arms and hips and feet were trained to tell the stories of the people—their gods, their origins, their voyages and exploits and affairs of the heart—and keep them alive from one generation to the next. Hula was the centerpiece of traditional culture, just as it has been the centerpiece of the current cultural renaissance. So any place dedicated to the deity of hula had probably been chosen with considerable care.

According to the famous myth of Pele and Hi'iaka, this is where the high chief Lohi'au sat drumming for some dancers, when his compelling rhythms were heard by Pele, the volcano goddess, from her fiery home in Puna, on what is now called the Big Island.

Drawn toward the sound, Pele's spirit-body traveled north from island to island until she reached the *hālau hula*, where the handsome chief was instantly smitten by her great beauty. In his nearby house they spent three days together, then Pele's spirit-body left Kaua'i and returned home. Unable to get Lohi'au out of her mind, she sent a younger sister, Hi'iaka, on a mission to bring him to her.

Thus begins a complex epic of high adventure, love and rivalry, death and transformation. One of the Pacific's great legend cycles, the story of Pele and Hi'iaka links Hā'ena in the far north with the Big Island's active crater region in the far south, underscoring the significance of this old *hālau hula* in both the geography and the mythology of the Hawaiian chain.

From the grassy terrace, looking north, it is all blue

ocean, with nothing between this cliff and the Aleutians 2,400 miles away. Out of that infinity the swells roll toward you. Near shore, each rising edge becomes a pencil line across the blue, then breaks to gush over wet black rocks directly below, where the inshore swirl is turquoise.

My dancer friend had told me that she and her troupe once flew here from the Big Island, 350 miles south and east, to pay their respects to the goddess who first brought hula to Hawai'i. They began by dipping themselves in those waters, said to be healing and purifying for performers. They entered from Kē'ē Beach, and then, with their leis and skirts and ankle-ferns dripping, they climbed barefoot up the trail and made an offering of their dance.

In the wall behind the platform there are niches and small ledges where the most recent offerings could be seen, nontraditional, left by visitors paying their respects—a bunch of wild daisies, a circular head lei of close-pressed flowers, a piece of star fruit, a polished *kukui* nut, a fresh mango wrapped in a ti leaf.

Root tendrils dangled from above. Higher up, ti plants and papaya trees had sprouted from the cliff. The plant-layered wall, with its natural altar, is framed by two narrow canyons that shape a bowl, a cathedral of eroded lava. The two canyon jungles, thick with palms and more papaya and ironwood and ferns, slope steadily toward the peaks and scoured ridges that cup around behind.

One bold spire seems to rise like an obelisk, and above these peaks, the clouds spilled seaward, gauzy, urgent clouds floating down from Mount Wai'ale'ale, ten miles away, known to be the wettest spot on earth.

As these clouds poured over the ridges, they mirrored the panorama of rolling surf. Their gliding shadows could also change the colors of the sea, from turquoise to diamond blue to cobalt. I felt I knew then why dancers had been coming there for centuries to commune with hula's guiding spirit. I saw what my friend had meant by "sources."

The changing water, the spilling clouds, the creased and jagged peaks behind were all bathed in an uncanny liquid light. A wind swept down to riffle the palms and the papaya trees, and the whole place had come alive, moving in its own kind of elemental dance.

James D. Houston is the author of *In the Ring of Fire: A Pacific Basin Journey*, published by Mercury House, and the award-winning novel *Continental Drift*, reprinted last fall in the new California Fiction Series from the University of California Press. He lives in Santa Cruz. This article originally appeared on the Internet on the web magazine *Salon*. His story "The Woman Who Talked to Rocks" appears in *Hawai'i's Best Spooky Stories: The Original* (first published in 1996 under a different title).

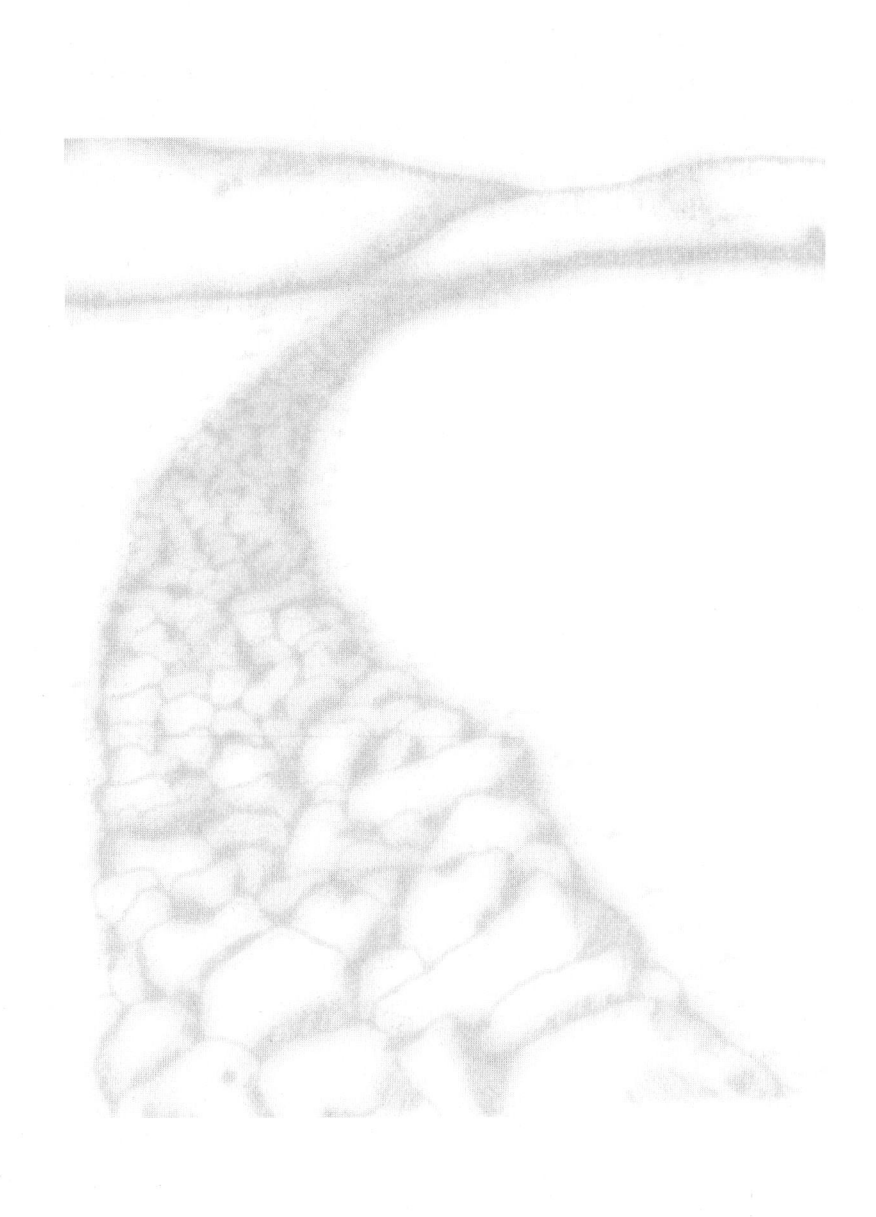

Sacred Places

Sacred Fishing Grounds

Quest for Honopū

The Red Hand of Wahiawa

When you go fishing at night in Hawai'i there are certain things to remember besides your bait and tackle. You must always know where you are; the sea cliffs are steep and the waves can be deadly. Sometimes, your favorite fishing spot may deliver more excitement than you thought possible, as the daughter of a dearly departed Kaua'i angler discloses in her spooky memoir . . .

Sacred Fishing Grounds

by Joyce Guzman

This story was told to me by my dad—God rest his soul—when I was a little girl, about a night he went fishing and finally understood the reason for a mystery and occurrence that didn't even rattle him.

My dad was a fisherman. All dads in Hawai'i, whether they held another steady job or not, were still considered fishermen. Even though my dad was a stevedore and made good money, we still ate fish every day until it was coming out of our ears. But I loved it, although I never had the pleasure to sink my teeth into a nice thick, juicy steak or baked chicken with all the trimmings. We had fried fish, fish soup, dried fish, and even raw fish. Makes for good health and nice complexions, I would say—wouldn't you?

Anyway, Dad used to love fishing. Day or night, he couldn't get enough of it. One night he decided to go fishing down at Salt Pond toward the end of the road, where he would throw in his line and just kick back in the car waiting for a bite.

This one night he parked his old '50 Chevy on the edge of a small ledge where the sand and rocks meet the water's edge. I would say this ledge was about five feet high if you were standing on the sand looking up at his car, and the ledge had broken off, exposing a lot of red dirt and grass on top of the ledge where his car was parked.

Well, he threw in his line and hooked his pole to the bumper of the Chevy, and attached a bell to the pole to let him know when he had a bite—that is, in case he fell asleep. He fell asleep all right, only to be awakened by an abrupt shaking and moving of the car and the bell ringing like crazy.

He got up, looked around, but saw no one. He got out of the car and saw the car still rocking and shaking. It finally dawned on him that he must be on sacred ground or on an ancient grave and it wanted him to GET OFF NOW and move on.

With that, he calmly gathered his pole and said, "I'm sorry, I didn't know I was on top of you. I will go now."

When Dad told me this story, I could not believe how calm he was. He understood and respected the grounds where ancient graves once were and he always taught us that this is the way it always has to be.

Years went by, and we continued to camp down at Salt Pond, except we camped at the other end, where there were beautiful white sands and shrubbery that made a wonderful place to camp and play.

One night all of us kids decided we were going to walk the beach all the way to the end to look for seashells.

The night before had been a little scary because we all heard someone running up and down outside of our camps, but saw no one there. The day brought new and different feelings toward the night. So we took our flashlights and went on to find seashells.

As I was walking, I spotted a shell that I could not quite make out. It looked so different that I had to pick it up to get a closer look. At first I thought it was a broken *puka* shell, and then I realized I had found a human tooth; in fact it was a molar.

Later, I found more and I started to feel a little eerie about it. I threw the teeth back on the sand, and believe me, I couldn't wash my hands enough to get the feel out of them. It scared me to think I had actually picked up human teeth.

We walked farther toward the end where Dad had parked his car years ago, and I couldn't help but look up at the spot. To my amazement, I was staring at a skull with two bones crisscrossed in front of it. It was sitting smack in the middle of the ledge of red dirt where Dad had parked his car that night years ago.

The wind and rain had washed some of the ledge away and exposed this grave that no one knew ever existed.

We all ran back to tell my dad, and he and his friend, Chu, went out the next morning to give it a proper burial. Dad finally had proof that years before he was sitting on top of this ancient grave. He was glad he was able to give the skull and bones a decent burial.

Joyce Guzman, born on Kaua'i, graduated from Waimea High in 1961. She now lives in Dana Point, California, where she works for JCP as a makeup artist and sales associate. She also contributed "A Moonlit Night at Anahola," "Grandma's Finally at Rest," and "The Grandma Who Talked to Ghosts."

Years ago, I set out on an inaugural flight to the "forbidden island" of Niʻihau on a Twin Otter, a most airworthy plane, and the wind came up so strong and the turbulence became so violent, the pilot was forced to turn back and put down safely back at Kauaʻi's Princeville Airport. Hawaiʻi reveals itself slowly, if at all, to all of us. Many folks think they can just go to certain sacred places without asking permission. Almost always they are lucky—the islands open up to them—but sometimes they are repelled by circumstances beyond their control, as this first-time visitor to Kauaʻi discovered on her . . .

Angela Dollar

Quest for Honopū

There is a brand of bottled water in Hawai'i called Menehune, named for the magical creatures that once lived on Kaua'i. The label on the water bottle depicts a jovial Menehune—short, rotund, and smiling like a Keebler elf on shift at the cookie factory. Due to the fact that they were small people, the Menehune are typically depicted as feisty little trolls or mischievous magical midgets at best.

Well, at least they got the magic part right. I was told that the name Menehune was originally drawn from *manahune*, the word *mana* referring to what the Hawaiians believe is the source of spiritual energy.

Apparently, the Menehune's abilities to channel and direct *mana* allowed them to perform feats that average mortals could not. Their smaller stature was a reflection of this—the Menehune possessed physical strength many times stronger than that of humans. It was with this power that they were able to lift the large boulders they used to construct a civilization in the valley of Honopū.

At least, that's the story I was told before I set out to explore Honopū. Now, I don't know what to believe. I only know that some thing, some force, still guards the valley of mystery and power.

Honopū is nestled in one of the most private corners of Nā Pali Coast on the north shore of Kauaʻi; it is accessible only by water. Even the arduous eleven-mile Kalalau Trail, the only foot passage into Nā Pali's tropical playground, will bring you only as far as Honopū's neighboring valley, Kalalau.

From the farthest end of Kalalau Beach, Honopū is still just out of grasp, although tides and fair seas allow strong swimmers to reach Honopū now and then. But it is a serious undertaking, and Honopū is choosy about who it allows to enter. That's how I feel now.

Honopū's gateway, as it has been described to me, is its arch—a giant rainbow of rock that crowns the beach. By climbing this archway, the few and the brave may enter the hanging valley that is the land of the Menehune.

While the dream of that adventure remains in my mental closet for another day, the desire just to see Honopū, to catch a glimpse of the mystical place, has gnawed at me since I heard of it. It wasn't until my last visit to Kalalau that I was given an opportunity.

I was on Kalalau Beach in the fading sunlight, watching the overture to what would soon be another spectacular sunset, when I noticed that the tide was out and the caves were exposed. There are two sea caves just around the far point of Kalalau Beach, and it is just past these caves where one might catch a glimpse of the elusive Honopū.

My boyfriend, Tom, our friend Jonathon, and I blazed a trail down the beach. There we definitely shared an air of excitement, but as we rounded the point I began to sense something and slowed my pace.

I looked out to the surf break, not far off from the

slender finger of beach we were now walking next to the rocky cliff sides. It struck me as both beautiful and chaotic, and I was awash in a daze of sheer awe and creeping foreboding.

The first sea cave was not far past the point. It was deep but not very tall, sculpted by the hands of the sea. I looked out to the ocean once more, and watched it crash and churn. I felt as if I were being let in on a secret performance, to observe the ocean at its choreographic best.

It occurred to me that I was a guest here, where the rocks and the waves had daily meetings, and that my pursuit of Honopū might not be on the agenda.

I knew the ocean might twist in a surprise finale.

The waves were building, coming from all directions, and suddenly I knew what that finale would be. The tide would be coming in. Quickly. I advanced to the mouth of the second cave to alert Tom and Jonathon to the developing critical conditions. We still had a skinny stretch of beach to cross back over before returning to the open Kalalau Beach.

Inside the cave, they were splashing around in ankle-deep water, oblivious to what the ocean had been telling me. As I made eye contact with Tom, a sweeping wave ran into the cave and pulled each of us off our feet. What had been ankle-deep water moments before now was up to our waists. My legs fluttered underwater like seaweed in the strong current. Not hesitating now, I looked at Tom and yelled, "Let's get the hell out of here!"

As soon as I had regained footing, I instinctively began to run for it. But the sand was soft and wet and pulled me in deep, so that running was virtually out of the question.

Looking out across the water, I could see the sets of waves, big and foamy, lined up to come onshore. Their opaque sandy hue was like a billboard that read HEAVY CURRENT.

I watched the next wave come crashing onto the shore, right over the heads of Tom and Jonathon in the cave. My stomach dropped. For a brief moment, as the wave scoured the entire cave, I feared they might be taken up with it and smashed against the rocky face of the cave. Tom must have anticipated it too, for seconds later I saw his head pop up with an arm extended to brace himself from a potential collision. The wave took him within inches of a jutting rock formation. Jonathon, too, popped up and narrowly avoided disaster. I didn't have to say it again; I turned on my heel as soon as I knew they were okay and ran for it. Sufficiently convinced, they got the hell out of there too.

Back in the safe arms of Kalalau Beach, the three of us had enough adrenaline coursing through our veins to power a college football team. We sat and watched the ocean for a while, quietly contemplating its mysterious, passionate, forbidding ways.

I thought of the land of Honopū, still a world away. I knew that, as there is for so many things in these magical islands, there must be a reason why Honopū can not yet be revealed to me. This had been a test. And when I return to find Honopū, I can only expect to be tested again.

Quest for Honopū *139*

Angela Dollar quit her job making backpacks in a small town near the Canadian border and set off to Kaua'i to, in her words, "travel with the wind for a while. Every day here is a living adventure—a writer's dream." She has contributed articles to the *San Juan Island Sounder*, worked as a cocktail waitress in Skagway, Alaska, and continues to wander and write. She also contributed "On Polihale Where Spirits Leap."

Her name tag said "Lani," and she had a big smile, rare for an airport car rental counterperson, but this was Hawai'i, Kailua-Kona International Airport, and Lani is Hawaiian. As we filled out the car rental agreement, Lani asked what I did, and when I told her, she said, "Eh, I got one story," and proceeded to tell me about . . .

The Red Hand of Wahiawa

LANI DONOVAN

We were picking up guava in Wahiawa, past the first bridge going to the Dole tourist place. This happened about thirty years ago. My baby was six to nine months old, and now she's like twenty-nine, so this is not a really old, old story, but it's true. My husband, well, really, my ex-husband, was picking up guava in one particular area, and I stood up above watching him and all the other people pick up guavas.

Instead of picking guavas off the ground like the other people, my husband pulled the branch down, and as he pulled the branch down he began shaking the limbs.

And then the tree started shaking.

I looked again. I saw him pull the branch down again and then let go. He turned around, walked around some like something hit him, and started walking up to where I was.

He came up and said he felt something rolling down his cheek. When he turned around, I saw a big red hand mark on his face. A big red hand mark on the left side of his face. And blood was running out of his ear—running down his cheek. And his eardrum was ruptured.

When I saw that, I knew what it was.

We went home right away and I called the

hoʻoponopono lady who lived in Wahiawa and she told us what we were supposed to do. She said we were supposed to go back there and apologize because it was a sacrificial area. Old Hawaiians had sacrifices there. We had disturbed the area and if we didn't go back I would lose my family, my children—my whole family.

The *hoʻoponopono* lady told me my husband would give me a bad time at the time, and he did. He refused to go back. He said it was pretty stupid. He's a *haole*, and he said he didn't believe any of that old Hawaiian stuff.

But finally I got him to go, and we went back together and we apologized. And we were afraid because we didn't know what to expect. But the *hoʻoponopono* lady said everything would be okay because we didn't do it on purpose or to make trouble and as long as we apologized everything would be fine. And it was, but my husband was suffering for a long time, and to this day, he has a scar on his eardrum.

We went to the doctor. My husband told the doctor that the door hit his ear. The doctor looked at him funny and said, "You can tell me the truth how this happened." The doctor knew better.

And then I told him the truth. And he said, "I don't believe in that but I've heard stories and I believe what you are saying is true because I know the eardrum is busted."

It wasn't the spirits upset over picking the guava, no way. It was over disturbing the sacred place. We could have taken all the guava, no problem. We should have asked permission to be in that space.

I don't think too many people know of that area. Kids who live around that place today, if they don't know about this, that can happen to them.

And if I was to go over there again, I would know about where the area is, but because I know I won't go there. I stay away. I never went back. After we apologized I never went back there to pick guava again. You learn your lesson.

Lani Donovan, formerly of Oʻahu, is a counter clerk at Dollar rental car at Kailua International Airport, Big Island of Hawaiʻi. When she goes picking up guava now, no matter where, she always asks permission.

Heiau

Hawaiian Methods of Interment

Incident at ʻIliʻiliʻōpae Heiau

Something Awful Happened

With old Hawaiian graves yielding skeletons in Waikīkī and burial caves being exposed on Oʻahu's North Shore, I decided it's high time to investigate Hawaiian burial practices. At the Hawaiʻi State Library one afternoon I came upon this true spooky story, written in 1825 by the missionary William Ellis, entitled . . .

Hawaiian Methods of Interment

We were desirous of witnessing the interment of the person who died last night, but were disappointed; it was, as most of their funerals are, performed in secret.

A few particulars, relative to their mode of burying, we have been able to gather from the people of this place and other parts of the island. The bones of the legs and arms, and sometimes the skull, of their kings and principal chiefs, those who were supposed to have descended from the gods, or were to be deified, were usually preserved, as already noticed.

The other parts of the body were burnt or buried, while these bones were either bound up with cinet, wrapped in cloth, and deposited in temples for adoration, or distributed among the immediate relatives, who, during their lives, always carried them wherever they went.

This was the case with the bones of Tamehameha; and it is probable that some of his bones were brought by his son Rihoriho on his recent visit to England, as they supposed that so long as the bones of the deceased were revered, his spirit would accompany them, and exercise a supernatural guardianship over them.

They did not wash the bodies of the dead, as was the practice with some of the South Sea Islanders. The bodies of priests, and chiefs of inferior rank, were laid out straight, wrapped in many folds of native tapa, and buried in that posture; the priests generally within the precincts of the temple in which they had officiated.

Different Burial Methods

A pile of stones, or a circle of high poles, surrounded their grave, and marked the place of their interment. It was only the bodies of priests, or persons of some importance, that were thus buried.

The common people committed their dead to the earth in a most singular manner. After death, they raised the upper part of the body, bent the face forwards to the knees, the hands were next put under the hams, and passed up between the knees, when the head, hands, and knees were bound together with cinet or cord. The body was afterwards wrapped in a coarse mat, and buried the first or second day after its decease.

They preferred natural graves whenever available, and selected for this purpose caves in the sides of their steep rocks, or large subterranean caverns.

Sepulchral Caves

Sometimes the inhabitants of a village deposited their dead in one large cavern, but in general each family had a distinct sepulchral cave. Their artificial graves were either simple pits dug in the earth, or large enclosures.

One of the latter, which we saw at Keahou, was a space surrounded with high stone walls, appearing much like an ancient *heiau,* or temple.

We proposed to several natives of the village to accompany us on a visit to it, and give us an outline of its history; but they appeared startled at the thought, said it was a *wahi ino* (place evil), filled with dead bodies, and objected so strongly to our approaching it, that we deemed it inexpedient to make our intended visit.

Occasionally they buried their dead in sequestered places, at a short distance from their habitations, but frequently in their gardens, and sometimes in their houses. Their graves were not deep, and the bodies were usually placed in them in a sitting posture.

BURIALS ARE SECRET AND WITHOUT CEREMONY

No prayer was offered at the grave, except occasionally by the inhabitants of Oahu. All their interments are conducted without any ceremony, and are usually managed with great secrecy.

We have often been surprised at this, and believe it arises from the superstitious dread the people entertain respecting the places where dead bodies are deposited, which they believe resorted to by the spirits of those buried there.

Like most ignorant and barbarous nations, they imagine that apparitions are frequently seen, and often injure those who come in their way.

Their funerals take place in the night, to avoid observation; for we have been told, that if the people were to see a party carrying a dead body past their houses, they would abuse them, or even throw stones at them, for not taking it some other way, supposing the spirit would return to and fro to the former abode of the deceased by the path along which the body had been borne to the place of interment.

BONES THROWN TO PELE AND THE SHARKS

The worshippers of Pele threw a part of the bones of their dead into the volcano, under the impression that the spirits of the deceased would then be admitted to the society of the volcanic deities, and that their influence would preserve the survivors from the ravages of volcanic fire.

The fishermen sometimes wrapped their dead in red native cloth, and threw them into the sea, to be devoured by the sharks.

Under the influence of a belief in the transmigration of souls, they supposed the spirit of the departed would animate the shark by which the body was devoured, and that the survivors would be spared by those voracious monsters, in the event of their being overtaken by any accident at sea.

The bodies of criminals who had broken tabu, after having been slain to appease the anger of the god whose tabu, or prohibition, they had broken, were buried within the precincts of the *heiau*.

The bones of human sacrifices, after the flesh had rotted, were piled up in different parts of the *heiau* in which they had been offered.

English missionary William Ellis (1794–1872), a pioneer of printing in the Pacific, was sent in 1816 to Polynesia as a nonconformist missionary. He set up at Tahiti the first printing press in the South Seas, and served as a missionary in Hawaiʻi from 1822 to 1823, where he developed a form of writing for the Hawaiian language, and authored numerous journals including *Narrative of a Tour Through Hawaii, or Owhyee, With Observations on the Natural History of the Sandwich Islands, and Remarks on the Manners, Customs, Traditions, History, and Language of Their Inhabitants*, 3rd edition. London: H. Fisher, 1827.

Incident at *'Ili'ili'ōpae* Heiau 151

A minor trespass on an ancient sacrificial *heiau* on the island of Moloka'i sets off a chain of events that stains the ocean blood-red on an otherwise perfect day in Paradise in this . . .

Incident at 'Ili'ili'ōpae Heiau

Rick Carroll

Michael and I wanted to see 'Ili'ili'ōpae, the great Moloka'i *heiau*, where Hawaiian *kahuna* practiced rites of human sacrifice only 150 years ago.

We hired a car at Ho'olehua Airport and drove to Kaunakakai, once the summer place of King Kamehameha V, now only a sun-bleached cluster of clapboard stores covered by fine red dust. It was around Christmas, so icicle lights twinkled in 82-degree heat, and shops displayed cheery Santa masks.

At Misaki's Market, where antlered deer-head trophies guarded aisles of rusty canned goods, we found shelves stripped bare by a run on fresh goods. A clerk said seas in Kaiwi Channel were so high, boats couldn't reach Moloka'i.

We grabbed the last six-pack of Hinano and local venison jerky and headed down two-lane King Kamehameha V Highway past tranquil fishponds big as lakes, protected from the sea by coral stone walls.

We passed a white clapboard church bathed in a bold ray of light, with a graveyard full of black cats prowling tombstones draped by dead flower lei, and drove by a roadside sign indicating a 1927 plane crash.

We added the church and crash site to our list of

unusual visitor attractions on Moloka'i, which already included the flirty mahus at Pau Hana Inn, a huge penis-shaped boulder known as the Phallic Stone, and the mule ride down the world's steepest sea cliffs to see the old leper colony at Kalaupapa.

Where the island became lush, green, and tropical, we turned *makai*, down an unmarked red dirt road, and entered the cool, shady oasis of Mapulehu, one of Hawai'i's botanical wonders.

Someone long ago had planted a specimen grove of mango trees by the sea, and the many varieties—Atkins, Haden, Ataulfo, Keitts, and Cebu, to name but a few—flourished to create a dreamy *Green Mansions*-like place steeped in perfume so strong it stung our eyes.

Under the sheltering mango trees, we stood in half-light, blinking, just as two galloping horses rounded a corner pulling a wagonful of screaming children who at first looked terrified, then delighted. The wagonful of children disappeared in fine red dust that settled on green mango trees and all over us, and a smiling woman appeared and welcomed us with a warm *aloha*.

I've forgotten her name, but not what she told us—that Mapulehu once was a *pu'uhonua*, a place of refuge, where in ancient savage days an errant subject could avoid death by gaining access. The location was appropriate, since 'Ili'ili'ōpae, the biggest, oldest, most famous *heiau* on Moloka'i, that served as a kind of school of sorcery, was a short hike up the hill.

We had missed the wagon to the *heiau*, the Hawaiian woman said, but we could go on foot if we liked. She pointed *mauka* toward cloud-spiked Mt. Kaunolu, the

4,970-foot island summit, and issued a caveat: "If you see a rainbow over the valley, look out for the *waikōloa*," she said.

"What's the *waikōloa*?" I asked.

"A hard, wet wind that comes suddenly down the valley," she said, and disappeared, like that, in the mango grove.

We set out on the upland trail through a *hale koa* thicket spiked by Java plum trees and, after passing an abandoned house, arrived hot, sweaty, and light-headed at the *heiau* just as the children were hiking back to the wagon. The *heiau* would be ours alone to explore.

I had read *Molokai: A Site Survey*, by Catherine C. Summers, the definitive work on the island's archaeology, so I knew the stone altar was 22-feet high, but no words prepared me for the bulky reality.

Long as a football field, nearly three stories high, 'Ili'ili'ōpae looks more like an early Roman fortification than a Hawaiian temple of doom. It rises in four tiers on the hill overlooking the green mango grove and four fishponds on the south shore of the island. What I found most amazing is that boulders big as Volkswagens had been fitted together in such tight array that the temple had been held together for centuries not by mortar, but by its own mass.

Originally, the *heiau* was three times larger, according to 'Ōhulenui, who grew up in the shadow of the temple and was ninety-six years old in 1909, when he was interviewed by archaeologist John F.G. Stokes, then director of the Bishop Museum. The *heiau* once stretched 920 feet across both east and west arms of Mapulehu Stream.

Temple rocks were swept away in legendary storms, or were taken to build the coast highway and bolster fishpond walls, which may account for appearances of the squid woman, and frequent auto fatalities.

Legend says 'Ili'ili'ōpae was built in one night by a human chain of ten thousand men who passed rocks hand over hand up and over the spine of the long narrow island from Wailau Valley, ten miles away over a precipitous trail across the nearly mile-high island. Each received one shrimp (*'ōpae*) and some rice in exchange for the rock (*'ili'ili*).

Even under the glaring tropic sun in full light of day the *heiau* is a very eerie place. Heat waves shimmer off the flat surface rocks. The walls vibrate with *mana* strong enough to lean on. I felt like someone was watching me.

I had read accounts of what happened here long ago, how people were summoned by the beating of drums and loud shouting on the 24th to the 27th day of the moon, when the sacrificial victim was carried into the temple tied to a scaffold. Victims were always men, not young virgins, and they were strangled while priests sat on *lauhala* mats watching silently. Victims never were buried, always burned; there was no boneyard, only ashes.

Against all advice, I stepped out on the *heiau*, walked right out on the flat table-sized rocks to gain a sense of the whole. I meant no disrespect. I only wanted to get closer—to what?—the primal past, the secrets of the *heiau*. I don't know what compelled me to commit this minor trespass. I knew better, and yet I kept walking out farther on the *heiau*, drawn by something larger than my curiosity.

Midway across the *heiau*, I grew dizzy in the hot sun. It beat down on me and radiated up from the rocks. I decided to turn back and slipped ankle deep between a rock that opened and closed around my ankle. Something had hold of me.

Unsure what happened, I yelled for help, but even as Michael turned around to see me trapped on the *heiau*, the rock moved again and my wedged ankle was free. I tiptoed across the *heiau* and touched down on terra firma. No spirits, no ghosts; only a misstep on a wobbly rock.

We scrambled up the steep *mauka* ridge, attempting to get a picture, but the *heiau* proved too big for our simple lenses. Only an aerial shot would capture the full image in proper context.

I looked up toward the mountain and saw a rainbow beginning to appear and remembered what the Hawaiian woman said.

"It's the *waikōloa!*" I shouted, as the rainbow grew bigger and brighter. Michael and I decided to hurry back down the dry streambed and reached the sheltering mango grove as hard rain came pelting down.

That afternoon on Moloka'i a flash flood sent water coursing once again through Mapulehu's dry streambed, and rain pounded the hot rocks of the ancient sacrificial *heiau*, sending up clouds of steam, and the fresh water seeped around old smooth stones and trickled down to the soul of the temple, where relic ashes repose.

Water ran through the rocks and across the highway and into the mango grove and over the beach, and it turned the fishponds and the sea blood-red. The entire south coast of Moloka'i was stained red the next morning when Michael and I flew back to Honolulu.

I don't know if one thing had to do with the other. I am sure it was all coincidence. I do know it was good to visit 'Ili'ili'ōpae *heiau*, but it was better to leave.

Rick Carroll is the creator of the *Hawai'i's Best Spooky Tales* series.

Young, educated, sophisticated, Hawai'i-born, she always seemed most unlikely to encounter something supernatural. Which is why I was so surprised to hear her *heiau* story. I still don't know the whole story, and probably never will, but it doesn't matter. What matters is that . . .

Something Awful Happened

Rick Carroll

I first heard about the incident at lunch one day in Chinatown. We met at Indigo and as we chopsticked through Monk's Buns and Green Papaya Salad, I asked if she had ever experienced anything out of the ordinary while growing up in Hawai'i. She turned pale as the rice on my plate.

"Omigod, yes," she said. "When I was in college, there was this girl and none of us liked her and one night we went and painted her name on a *heiau*, and . . . "

She paused.

"Yes?"

"It was terrible," she said.

"What happened?"

"I'm ashamed to admit it."

"Admit what?"

"Well, it was just a college prank, but after we painted her name on the *heiau* . . . "

"Yes, go on."

"Something awful happened to her."

"Really? Tell me. What happened?"

"No, I can't," she said. "It's too spooky."

We ate lunch and talked of other things that day, but the next time we met, I asked her to tell me the rest of the story. "Oh," she said, "I just can't. It's still too, you know, still too scary."

Her reluctance puzzled me, especially since the incident at the *heiau*, and the unspeakable result, whatever it was, occurred years ago, but I decided not to press the issue.

Now, whenever I see my friend, I always wonder what happened to the girl nobody liked and how a name painted on a *heiau* could cause something awful to happen, but I don't ask anymore. I don't really need to know. In Hawai'i there are secrets that should be kept.

Rick Carroll is the collector and editor of *Hawai'i's Best Spooky Tales*.